I0773442

MIDNIGHT LOVE POTION

Poetry and Prose

Marisa Loretta

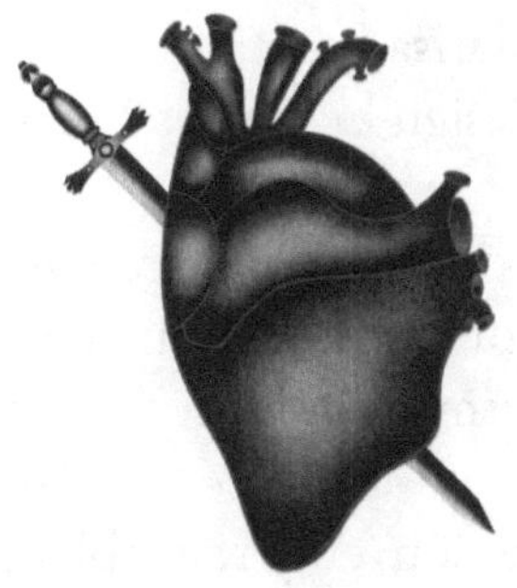

Copyright © 2022 by Marisa Loretta
Illustrations and cover design by Marisa Loretta

All rights reserved. This book and the accompanying illustrations may not be reproduced or distributed in any form whatsoever without clear, written permission from the author.

This book is a work of fiction. Any resemblance to real persons or events is entirely coincidental.

ISBN: 979-8-9872450-0-2 (paperback)
ISBN: 979-8-9872450-1-9 (eBook)

www.marisaloretta.com

Table of Contents

Part I: Fine Arts   *1*

Part II: Regency   *33*

Part III: Fantasy   *74*

Part IV: Romance   *148*

Part V: Reflection   *208*

*This is my last love letter to you, though some would call it a
confession. I suppose both are a sort of gentle violence, putting
down in ink what scorches the air when spoken aloud.*

—S.T. Gibson, *A Dowry of Blood*

Part II: Fine Arts

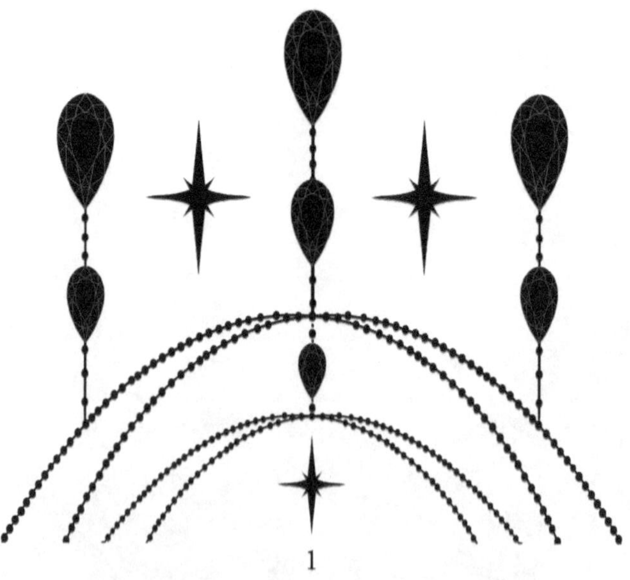

Cosmic Gift

The moon whispered her secrets to the dreamers
below, and we awoke poets
Though we are made of stardust and moonlight,
we do not shine as brightly
Our blood does not glow as the sky does; our
skin does not gleam in the dark
It is only the gift of poetry that allows us to truly
come alive, awakening us all
With the words we speak, the ones we inscribe,
the ones we keep for ourselves
In poetry, we are born anew, made of all that is
cosmic and nurtured by prose
The stars that crafted us were only given light by
holding the secrets of the sky
Once we learned those mysteries, once they were
softly spoken against our skin
Only then could we rival the luster of the stars
with our own splendor
The moon wept tears of prose onto the flesh of
romantics, and so poets they became
Poetry falls from their parted lips as naturally as
rain tumbles from a darkening sky
Hear them speak melodic words, bottle the
sound like light from a midsummer firefly
Read their odes with reverence and let their
verses become an unwavering part of you
Drink their words in with your ravenous, in-
finite soul, never with your shallow eyes
Poets are wholly consumed by their own poetry,
as if the prose is sewn into their skin
Expressive lyrics keep their hearts steadily
pounding, their blood passionately flowing
At last, when their poem is over and their
mouths delicately close, they will fade away
The poetry they cherished seeping from their
bodies, returning ever so softly to the moon

Chateau

A lofty chateau resides in the idyllic French countryside
Tepid rain patters against the high, slightly ajar windows
Thin curtains loosely tied back, lightly swaying in the wind
Warm, dreamy watercolors cascade down your fresh canvas
Paint finds a home on your tarnished, threadbare clothes
Your hands are never without a brush, itching to create
Golden sunlight peaks through darkening storm clouds
Gifting the most luminous light to bathe your work in

Escape into the world of art; immerse yourself in paint
Feel the brushstrokes as they lightly dance across your skin
Sense the restorative powers of art wash over your body
Realize, with a start, that dusk had long ago emerged
And now the moon will cast down its crystalline glow
Flooding the skylight, shining a beacon on your artwork
With the scent of paint whirling across the midnight air
And the otherworldly ecstasy within the heavenly sky
Feel a deep wave of contentment wash over your soul

The immense power that an evocative painting can hold
And the strength which art contains, is entirely therapeutic
It stays with you, lingering long after you finish crafting
It follows you into the dark and seeps into your dreams
Delight in the serenity you have been graciously gifted
And when a new day deigns to dawn over the chateau
Let that sense of harmony guide you while you create
And once again enter a realm of gentle inspiration

The Tale of Sorrow

Some libraries come alive with the collection of stories
That live within the array of books they humbly hold
Their tales bloom and burst with such joy and delight
Encapsulating the library in a comforting aura of awe

And yet that is not the case in this dwelling of horrors
This disturbing library is encased in complete darkness
And home to a miserable medley of moaning spirits
Here, books fall from shelves, brimming and buzzing
With terrible words that lie within their ancient pages
Ominous foreboding soaks into the dilapidated walls
Until the foundation falls, returning to bone-wet clay
Lights flicker frantically as vengeful ghosts pass by
Driving away any signs of hope and any signs of life

All the books in the library are saturated in total despair
All except for one, *The Tale of Sorrow*, never to be read
It does not merely contain sorrow; it is sorrow incarnate
Shunned, avoided like a deadly contagion, shrouded in dust
Unimaginable horrors lie within the haunting slew of pages
Slowly peel open the book and warily touch the cursed text
Let your eyes run over the words, and never again know elation
You will die as the story sinks its sharp teeth into your very soul
Damning you a spirit, doomed to haunt the library for an eternity
The Tale of Sorrow does not only force endless tears and tremors
It steals your breath, takes your life, and waits for its next victim

Song of the Sky

Shattered, lying on the unforgiving floor, defeated, and so tired
Resting her frail hands above her head to try and ease the agony
The throbbing pain she feared would never relent, not in this life
Blood streaming from her nose, giving her lips a strawberry tint
Mouth tasting of copper from her blood and salt from her tears

Distantly she heard angelic music floating down from elsewhere
Mercifully, her weeping halted as she began to listen in rapt awe
Maybe a soft and airy cloud knew of her torment and suffering
And arranged to send her something harmonious to lift her spirits
To whoever gave her this gift of music, she was deeply indebted

The expressive sounds of violins, the rhythmic flow of piano keys
The pulsing beat of drums and the dulcet tune of unearthly harps
Hauntingly harmonious melodies flowed naturally into her heart
Soon the blood and tears and distress covering her face vanished
And as the music soared within her, turning her pain into pleasure
For once, she was able to slumber, able to dream so very sweetly

Ode to Literature

Leather-bound volumes of tale after tale, bursting with prose
Exquisitely knotted with ribbons colored the shade of primrose
Aged, worn pages that never fail to make us weep and shiver
Teeming with promises that only illusory stories can deliver
Divine are the contents of a book, inundated with such appeal
Capable of stitching the open wounds that we never could heal
We are tethered to the Earth by the very soil that sprouts flowers
Just as we are tethered to our souls by literature's potent powers
Encase our bodies tightly within an invigorating bundle of text
Let us remain inside the story, wondering what will come next
Drown us deeply into a tranquil river overflowing with fiction
Sail us to another world where we may live without restriction
Let us lay in a field of lilies, sunbathing in the summertime air
Allow us to accept a crown of golden roses that we proudly wear
Watch us become dragonflies, hovering over a shimmering creek
Delight in the wonders of these vast worlds, filled with mystique
Literature stays with us long after the story has come to an end
Read, and let the fracturing cracks within our souls start to mend

Poetry and Peace

Poetry should soften the vitriol that haunts your body
It should plant novel seeds and shower down upon them
Calmly watering the perennial garden inside of your mind
Each word should allow a new flower of hope to blossom
Every page should pull out deeply rooted weeds of doubt
Prose must ignite your bones, inflame your bloodstream
Gently wrap around your organs, beat beside your heart
Only if the poem strikes true will it keep planting seeds
For your thoughts are now a string of enthralling words
Immortalized onto the page, forever ready to return to
Whenever your flowers need affection and attention

Poetry should invade your soul, piercing and penetrating
As if you were born with those exact words inside of you
Now, as you read, as you thoughtfully take in the prose
The words will return to your body, seamlessly fitting
As if you had been unknowingly saving space for them
You should gasp, panting in awe, completely speechless
For you cannot imagine how you have lived so very long
Without these words that so clearly belong only to you

Poetry should begin, each and every time, in the same way
With the pouring out of your private heart onto the page
Taking shape in the form of pleasing words and couplets
But it should end with others reading those same words
And feeling as if they are looking upon their own heart
As if the poet, all at once, reached deep inside of them
Past flesh and bones, and plucked out their soul to study
Poetry should put into words what they truly feel within
What they could never explain, though they urgently tried
As the reader gazes upon the page, they will feel at peace
They will feel honest harmony, perhaps, for the first time

Bleeding Canvas

Pierce my flesh until my arms run red with scarlet blood
Watch in a daze as the warm liquid coats my fingertips
Notice how closely it resembles thick, almost arterial paint
A bright shade so intense no other hue would do it justice
Pluck the bones from my skeleton; wield them as brushes
Use the walls near me as a canvas, for art knows no bounds
Pull my luminous hair straight from my skull; use it to blend
Cradle my pounding heart in your hands; roughly tear it open
Use it when my veins run dry and you are in need of more ink
Rip me apart; rupture my organs until the painting is finished
For there is nothing I would not sacrifice of myself for art
I would murderously melt myself down into a mere puddle
If I thought the wading waters of my body would be beautiful
I would walk into fire if I believed my ashes might glisten

Give your life to your craft; limitlessly offer it your skin and soul
And maybe enough of you will be left to finally enjoy your creation

Bookshop

When your flesh is coated in blood and your lungs have filled with water
Leave, drift far away from the horrors awaiting you where the sky is light
Wander deep into the forest until the daunting sunlight cannot reach you
With a shaky pulse and a failing heart, stumble upon a secluded book-shop
Hidden deep within the woods, nestled within an array of the lushest trees
Nymphs and pixies urge you to step closer toward this house of litera-ture
An escape, it seems, from the lesions on your skin, the toxins in your veins
In order to be rid of the metallic taste in your mouth, softly open the door

Feel the mystical aura that is blossoming within every brilliantly bound tale
Thousands of books sit packed upon shelves, showcasing their elegant spines
A fireplace, bordered by rows of sunbaked bricks, warms the soothing shop
This veritable reprieve from the revulsions of life is infused with such beauty
Walls are embellished with intricate, wistful murals depicting fictitious realms
Copper lanterns hang from vaulted ceilings, flooding the books in gilded light

The blissful bookshop will gladly indulge your each and every whim
and desire
Wipe the blood dripping down your nose, and yearn to be immersed in
literature
Watch as a pile of books effortlessly floats down into your open, waiting
arms
For this heavenly place, burrowed within an earthly forest, only wishes
to help
With a resonance of soft rain hitting the forest floor from just outside
these walls
Begin reading, and while you soak up each word as if you are starved for
fiction
Notice your skin is now pristine, beaming ethereally, in a way it never
has before
Cough up the water that had clogged your lungs, and begin breathing
much easier
Stay in the woodland acropolis as long as it takes for you to fully and
truly recover
Then, steady and sure, leave the sanctuary of the forest, and walk back
into the light

Destruction

Weeping to the mesmerizing beat of the music
Letting the sounds reverberate through my body
And though I tried to let the melody engulf me
Put me in a haze, distract me from my despair
The music only amplified what I was feeling within
With each lyric sung, with every note that passed
I felt myself rupturing piece by piece by piece
As if the melody seeped into every last inch of me
Into every place I believed was irreparably splintered
Pressing and pushing until the cracks gave way
Until my body gave itself over to the composition
Until I cataclysmically broke, falling to the floor
The sounds of the song filtered in completely
Washing over me, like an unrelenting wave
Once it devoured me, the cracks began to rebuild
The music acted as a salve, calming, repairing
Putting me back together, stronger than before
As the song gradually began to come to a close
Disappearing into a soon-to-be-silent atmosphere
My despair—not all, but enough—melted away too
Departing into the air beside the remnants of music
And when my tears once again begin to flow freely
Those remnants will band together, becoming whole
Forming a new song, ready to demolish me once more
And I will now be grateful for the destruction to come
For after the devastating break comes serene harmony
And as fleeting as that euphoric feeling of peace may be
It is always truly treasured and warmly welcomed within

Golden Library

Open the towering doors to the luxurious library and gasp at the sight
before you
Gold-covered walls, littered with blossoming ivy spreading from floor to
ceiling
Let your eyes be drawn to the domed skylight, giving a perfect view of
the baby blue sky
Sanctioning sunlight to bathe the countless books inhabiting the
breathtaking library
Stacked neatly in rows, shelves crafted from slabs of smooth marble
adorn the walls
Windows made from striking stained glass, cast the room in an array of
jewel tones
The peaceful space, though certainly grand in its décor, is not monu-
mental in size
And yet the other worlds residing within the books make it an infinite
place to be

Though the library is encased in shades of gold, the books remain plain
and simple
For the true beauty and grandeur lies inked within the wilted and wrin-
kled pages
Drag your fingers across the weathered spines; feel each one attempt to
pull you in
Let them succeed as you give yourself over to the wonders living within
those pages
Let each novel character inside your mind, to feel what they feel, see
what they see
Hear the rough gravel crunch beneath your feet as you run beside them
into battle
Feel the salty spray of the sea on your face as you stand on the prow of a
pirate ship
Lay in the green grass of another realm, wondering where your journey
will lead next
For within the walls of the golden library, anything and everything is
entirely possible

Poetic Love

She merely existed, and he began to overflow with prose
Fondly she touched his check, and he wept with gratitude
His soft lips sighed poetry against the column of her throat
And she reveled in the feel of his touch, the sound of his voice
No prose had ever before worshipped someone so selflessly
He spoke about her as if she was a star that fell from the sky
And he was lucky enough to catch her, cradle her in his arms
He made her feel as if she was an ethereal goddess of beauty
And he was a devious sinner who longed to repent before her
She was breathless, in constant awe of the poetry he produced
Her mind and body tripped over one another, desperate for more
More of his words or his mouth on hers, she could not be sure
She had never known that poems could affect her so physically
Each word made her shiver, tremble with glacial anticipation
Every line sent warmth through her bones and eased the chill
She felt the verses that rolled off his tongue bind to her flesh
Though she was sure her mind would never dare to forget them
History was being written on her arms, her stomach, her mouth
For the words he spoke were sure to be studied years from now
He took these words, birthed from his soul, wrought with devotion
And wrote them down, shyly saying, *a poem, for you, of our love*
As she attentively read each line, as her heart swelled and burst
She knew so clearly that he never needed to touch her body again
To feel overwhelmed with such heavenly ecstasy, all she needed
Were his words whispered into her ears, murmured to her mouth
And his romantically ardent poems covetously clutched in her hands

Sweet Words, Evil Men

Adoring love poems will never paint a true picture of men outside of
prose
In the real world of flesh and blood, men are rarely filled with such
kindness
They emanate a violent arrogance, one that is inherently ingrained
within them
Men nurture weeds of malevolence that wrap around their blackened
hearts
Sweet words spew from the sneering lips of evil men each unrelenting
day
Lies descend from their lips as often as snow descends during a winter's
night
But if their words were not coated in honey, we would not keep savor-
ing them

Men residing within poetry are saints whose backs are decorated with
ivory wings
Against your lips they murmur words sent straight from the mouths of
angels
Their hands hold bouquets of flourishing flowers they have picked just
for you
Your body is treasured, nurtured, cherished, without ever having to ask
They hold you in the dark, keeping you safe from what lies in the shad-
ows
In the light of day, they tuck your hair back to better gaze upon your
face

Men outside of prose are devils cleverly hiding their horns and pitch-
forks
With a harsh grip on your neck, they rasp out accusations, vile and
untrue
Their hands carry the ceaseless threat of pain and the promise of brutal-
ity
Taking your body as though it is their own, theirs to touch, to use, to
break
Abandoning you when night falls, leaving your sleeping body defense-
less
When the sun rises, their eyes are filled with nothing but cool indiffer-
ence

Let the men from poetry come to life; watch as they idolize and revere
And let them ruthlessly banish the men in reality, never to be seen again

Shakespeare's Sonnet

Shakespeare, eternally revered through his timeless prose
Feel his spirit guide you, be dauntless as you swiftly write
Let his immortal hand move yours as you begin to compose
Feel his sonnets flutter over your soul like an inspiring sprite

Read with the hunger of a starved bandit until you reach a break-
through
Inhale his fatal tragedies of passionate romances and ruinous conclu-
sions
Ingest his pages where tired hands are washed clean until they shine
anew
Weep, as poison is mournfully swallowed, fooled by deceptive delusions

But then pick up his books once more; read them until your eyes burn
For his poems are wholly transcendent and his plays enticingly divine
Trust in his brilliant mind, for Shakespeare wrote so we all could learn
So we all could drink in his tales as though they taste of ambrosial wine

Write a sonnet or two for Shakespeare and speak it to the sky
For he will be listening, a tear falling down his glittering eye

Twilight Melodies

In the near distance, past echoes of the revelries were scattered along twilight streets
An orchestra, grand and theatrical, played its symphony, captivating all who listen
Music flooded the air, drifting up to my balcony where I let the songs surround my body
Enveloping me in their mystifying ability to mend unspoken aches and unseen wounds
Melodies echoed loudly against my chest, pounding, nearly decimating my flesh and bone
Until they ran furiously through my bloodstream, racing, consuming me so fervently
That I thought they might soon begin to pour from my open mouth, bleed from my nose
Intense as this was, my body did not reject the music, it seemed to grasp onto it tighter
For if my body burst from the power of the music, what a melodic way it would be to go

My heart started to beat in time with the chorus, the music encouraging
it to thump faster
Moving through my body like a harsh hurricane, leaving no part of my
soul untouched
The music felt so intimately familiar as if to say, *I know, I am here, I am
listening now*
It allowed my mood to become tangible, something I could practically
feel, touch, see
Once I closed my eyes and gave myself over to the melody, nothing else
seemed to exist
As the music, regretfully, slowed down, the sounds grew dim as my
trembling eyes opened
And soon, I realized I felt lighter, just like the notes of a song floating
through the breeze
Grateful for the music that alleviated and eased my woe, though only
for one late night

Empty Mind

What if all my thoughts are gone now, having abandoned me
Freed from my mind, stuck inside the pages of this very book
I worry that with each word I write, my mind empties more
Until one day, millions of my words will be placed on paper
But my head will remain hollow, vacant of any and all thoughts
When a poet has nothing more to say, are they still named a poet?

Still, I must go on, rejoicing in the soothing power of the moon
Delight in the wind breezing by, revel in the steadily falling rain
Hoping that as I continue to live, continue to breathe, and to feel
My mind will once again fill until I have so much I need to say
That every sheet of paper in the world will still not seem enough
To contain the words whirling within my head, frantic to be freed
Continue writing I must, until the heaving pressure within lessens
Though this time, no hollow feelings will find me when I finish
Only a sense of enthusiasm will overwhelm me, to keep thinking
To keep writing and writing, for a poet once, remains a poet, always

Bathed in Prose

Bask in a beautiful, blissful world, bathed only in prose
Look on as heartfelt words freely fall from our mouths
Words are void of lies, for the truth is too sweet to hide
Feel every emotion along the soft curves of our bodies
Pleasure ripples through the earth, rooting into the dirt
True euphoria is as visible as the stars draped in the sky
Sorrows slowly drift out to sea to live among the naiads

Flowers grow until blossoming petals touch the moon
Feel a thorn stroke your skin, gasp as it does not pierce
Dulcet fruit tastes just like the heavenly blood of an angel
Aromas of lemon zest and orange blossom float in the air
Rain cascades down our bodies in a mist of pure pleasure
Live eternally within this undying realm crafted of poetry
And rejoice at what a breathtaking world it proves to be

Muses

Rarely is the product of inspiration as spellbinding as the spark of inspiration itself
The muse will continuously prove to be more stunning than the painting she inspires

She is more than art could ever hope to depict, for she lives, breathes, feels
Her skin is warm, her heart is beating, her face is sinfully, delectably flushed
Art is capable of so much, but it cannot hold you in the dark while you weep
The muse will speak, and her saccharine voice will fill your mind with designs
She will touch you, and you will rush to translate the feeling of her flesh onto canvas

The art you create will hold glimpses of her, so subtle, yet magnetic and mesmerizing
Though it will never truly capture her essence nor will it depict her captivating aura
Be inspired by the copious beauty of this world, the luminous stars, the blooming roses
But do not be disappointed when your art fails to seize the true glory that is your muse

Living Art

Sculpt me from marble as poets craft my mind
Scatter crimson chrysanthemums into my veins
Darken my hair from the most obsidian nights
Plunge a brush into starlight and paint my flesh
Paint my lips until they are as red as pomegranates
Dress me in satin made from strands of sunlight

Place me before the gods; let them look upon me
Pleased with their design, they wordlessly leave me
Exquisitely standing alone in such horrible solitude
So many meticulous touches went into my creation
Though I was sure I was designed for a violent end
Like a Greek tragedy that had not yet come to pass
So I waited alone, always on edge, always afraid

Living art, birthed for beauty, yet destined for ruin
The gods gazed down from above, hoping to use me
Wield my body as a weapon for their nefarious plots
With their distant eyes piercing me, I smiled sweetly
Reclaiming my power by displaying what they desired
My gaze hypnotic, my body alluring, my mind cunning
Born a blank canvas, but now the brush was in my hand

Opera House

The opera house sat abandoned, looking brittle and desolate
A suffocating gloom and hopelessness filled the stagnant air
As if the absence of music and tears and applause from within
Woefully left the exterior unable to display a façade of beauty
Inside, music within the walls could not be contained anymore
Instruments could wait no longer to revel within their own music
Timidly tuning themselves, though quickly regaining confidence
Rapidly, music miraculously began again, and the walls rejoiced

The instruments began playing with such conviction as if possessed
Yet the only spirits were those stifled inside the instruments themselves
The piano began to play a song with no pianist, no music, no audience
The keys moved fanatically, longing to sing their private melody aloud
The violins gracefully and expertly played song after song after song
Poised gracefully in the air, the bow moved quickly over the strings
A flute sang its ethereal song, the light tune gliding through the grand
space
The instruments had no need for an accompanist when they were first
played
With this exhilarating freedom, they undoubtedly have no need for one
now

Singing high toward the ceiling as the music seeped into the floorboards
The opera house began to restore itself, reignited by the sound of songs
If the absence of music had proven long ago to be detrimental, disas-
trous
Then the sudden reemergence of melodies such as these was revitalizing
The cracked door was lifted off of the ground until it sat back on its
hinges
Peeling paint barely coating the fractured walls became vivid and glossy
Droves of people, once again, lined up to hear the music playing within
The instruments, giving no mind to their new listeners, kept on playing
Vowing together to never again deprive the opera house of its music

Urgency to Write

Profusely dip your pen in ink, in mud, in your own blood
Feverishly compose with everything at your disposal
Stamp your words onto each surface you stumble upon
Carve your feathered quill into the ancient bark of trees
Nature itself will act as your immortal, unending paper
Write with a heated urgency, a steadfast desire to create
A poetic plea that will never be satiated, nor quelled
Until the emotions within your crowded, bursting mind
Are turned into lyrical sonnets and expressive stanzas
Do not risk hesitating nor lingering for even a moment
Until you are undeniably ready to lay your quill to rest

With a weary gaze, greedily ingest all you have written
Let your eyes ravenously roam over the saturated prose
Full of celestial witchcraft, guided by the stars and sky
Spellbinding stories brimming with romance and lust
Tales of dark creatures hungry only for flesh and gore
Feel dizzy, high off the fumes of bewitching fantasies
Seeping into the air with each mystical poem you pen
Look upon your creation and feel a sense of inspiration
Hope all others who simply happen upon your words
Will walk away with the want—the need—to write, too

Everlasting Poetry

Poetry falters over time, though the meaning will undeniably remain
When the inked pages wither away, lost to weather and time and age
The prose will never escape the sanctuary that is our boundless minds

When our pounding hearts are crushed, broken by betrayal and decep-
tion
Remember beloved tales of sincere romance, their healing aura a sooth-
ing balm
For poetry will never hesitate to sew and stitch the seams of our shat-
tered souls

So much will bleed from our brains as we travel through this long life
And yet, the words of great poets seem to forever find a place to stay
For their prose is too important, too embedded into our souls to forget

Goddesses of the future will humbly read our carefully crafted words
Just as we have read the words of those who distantly came before us
This cycle will continue, just as poetry will continue on, everlasting

Weeping Moon

Music of the night, melody of the dark, the moon sings a requiem of infinite grief
Lamenting over her cosmic isolation, the sound of her misery ricochets across the sky
Every wail and whine from her lips echoes like a symphony to the stars around her
Though laden with sorrow, her voice is as entrancing as the song of a hummingbird

The stars are too far, the sun is too hot, and the moon is left sequestered in the ether
Her crying does not relent, tears falling in perfect harmony with the refrain of her song
Her music and tears fall from the sky until they reach ivory clouds floating peacefully
Once they land, their immense weight proves to be far too much for the delicate clouds
Which have now turned grey and dense and so desperate to be rid of this woeful weight
And so, the tears, comprised entirely of the moon's song, fall in a downpour of despair

The moon watches with wide eyes as her melodic tears rain down upon
those below
Fearing her melancholy will permeate into their skin until they all begin
weeping too
Frantic with guilt, the moon looked on in horror and was astonished at
what she saw
People expressed such joy upon seeing the rain, hearing her song as it
landed on them
Her tempest of tears felt cool upon their warm skin, sounding glorious
as they listened
Looking up to the sky, they expressed thanks to the moon, grateful for
this gift of music

For the first time, the grieving moon did not feel so profoundly alone
within the universe
And though her thick tears still fell to the earth, and her melodious
wailing continued on
Now, no longer wretchedly lamenting, the moon wept from an unfa-
miliar sense of bliss

Fiction

Tales of mythology, classic literature, epic poems
All avidly absorbed by my hungry eyes day by day
Their words often feel so genuine, so tangibly true
As if I had lived alongside goddesses atop a cloud
Sat with queens upon their gilded, towering thrones
Felt the adoration within their consuming love stories
Touched and been touched by captivating characters
Wept and witnessed their fatal, terribly tragic endings
Feeling empty within when their stories come to a close
Longing to connect, to bond further, desperate for more

Wanting to bathe in the wells of antiquity, submerged
Yearning to converse with fabled, abandoned deities
Wishing to write alongside lost playwrights of before
Aching to swallow the blood of every neglected poet
Pining for them to show me their worlds once again
Please, invite me in, open your gates, beg me to stay
These stories have all placed a mark upon my flesh
A branding on my very soul, a scar made of fiction
And I will carry their words within every part of me
Through this weary life, and through every life after

Diamond Eyes

When this cold world is too much to bear
Look to literature for an escape, but first
Consider the fatal ends we so often read
Ponder if these tales might be enhanced
With an ending of such sweet joy instead

Cover our eyes with sparkling diamonds
Let us read of a more iridescent world
One where Orpheus did not turn around
And Euridice wept shocked tears of joy
Where Icarus suddenly grew true wings
And gently floated down to the ground
A world where Achilles joined no war
And lived a long life beside Patroclus
If we remove these kaleidoscopic gems
And consume such tales as they truly are
Where worlds are spun with fatal threads
And characters are plagued with heartache
Condemned for grief, yet gifted notoriety
Will these stories truly offer us a reprieve
From our own dreadful hurt and anguish
If that is what also lies within their pages?

Maybe it is best to keep the diamonds atop our eyes
Let them glisten, only for a little while longer still
For life is idyllic behind the lens of such ignorance
So adorn your face with crystals when you need to
Escape into a tale that will heal your damaged heart
Instead of breaking it further, until nothing remains

Fine Arts

Be wary of romantic and starry-eyed artists
They will see blood and think only of roses
Thorns will puncture their unblemished skin
Their blood will flow out in a river of love
And they will be thankful for the new paint
They will become infatuated at first glance
But will not survive the ensuing heartbreak
To cope, they will illustrate a perfect world
Free from flaws and flooded with pleasure
Reality will appear monotonous and bleak
So they will visit their calming art once again
And devour their vivid paints until they choke

Be cautious of dreamers with music in their blood
They will spot a seed of silence and bury it below
Within the depths of the dirt until it will not surface
They will ascend a steep mountain to the very peak
Trying to enter the celestial realm and reach the stars
Hoping to hear the rousing melodies within the sky
Only to slip, tumbling with their eyes peeled open
To see what refrains await them on the ground below
When they land, sirens will fill the air as their souls beam
For they knew in their hearts that music would find them

Be guarded of all writers, poets, authors
They will latch onto a spark of inspiration
And turn it into a blazing inferno of prose
They will lose themselves in another realm
Lost to the stacks of papers sitting before them
You will call out, yet they will never hear you
For the words they have so fanatically penned
Will hold them captive, perpetually confined
Though, the writers are enthusiastic prisoners
Who never desire to be relieved from their chains

Be warned of all who turn to the arts for an escape
Lost to their craft, they may never return to us
For blood will continue to pour from their flesh
Forever guiding their art, their song, their words
And as beautiful as their creations appear to be
Know that art comes with a price paved in sacrifice
For the fine arts take, almost as much as they give
And so many do not bat an eye at the costly toll
For it will all seem worth it in the very end

Part III: Regency

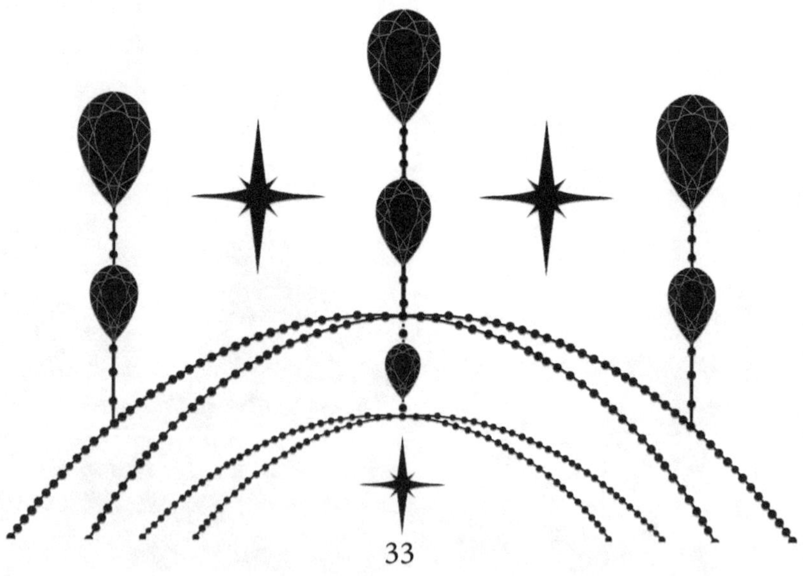

Castle of Midnight

The Castle of Midnight truly came alive once nightfall descended upon the land
Fog surrounded the palace in a haze whenever the luminous sun shone down
Only with the fading light and the promise of dusk did the exterior begin to glow
The deep ebony bricks sparkled under the stare of the moonlight night after night
Silver light, the same color as the moon herself, seeped into the walls of the castle
As though the ether had taken heaping handfuls of stardust into her supple hands
And sprinkled it carefully onto every window, every pillar, every door and lock
Now bathed in onyx and moonbeams, the castle was soon after gifted its name

Eerie gargoyles perched tall on the rooftop, looming over the expanse of the estate
Looking out toward the high hills sitting just beyond, strewn with nocturnal flowers
Plants that bloomed only under the watchful eye of the stars scattered in the sky
Moonflowers covered every inch of the botanical gardens, growing with fervor
Just off the side of the castle resided a stable, housing beloved and spirited mares
With hair the color of the shadows, they too rejoiced when darkness settled in
For they could witness the transformation of the palace before their very eyes

Within, the castle was regularly flooded with royalty, purring with sinful activity
Though those who passed by rarely longed to glide through the arched doorways
For the real beauty and excellence were in the mere foundation of the castle itself
Never before had an estate responded so resolutely to the presence of darkness
The Castle of Midnight did not question this inexplicable, mystical phenomenon
It merely waited in anticipation for the moon to take its place night after night
And when it did, the castle beamed so brilliantly, even the stars paled in contrast

Unexpected Love

I longed for a romantic, heady, all-consuming sort of love to find me
one day
Years passed, and that idealistic desire, that hope, began to fade, and
reality set in
I resigned myself to a life of ordinary liaisons at best, solemn solitude at
worst
Until one quiet evening I found myself walking alone in the outskirts of
my village
Picking flowers beside the road, gathering them in my arms to later
craft a bouquet
Suddenly a breeze lifted scattered leaves, and I heard a horse galloping
feverishly
I turned just in time to see someone quickly dismounting from their
noble steed
That someone, of course, was the last person I wanted to ever see or
utter a word to
My greatest foe and the root of my anguish, like a wasp relentlessly
circling me

I was a princess from South Court, and he was a duke from West Court
Suddenly standing before him, I smoothed my gown, feigning noncha-
lance
With a sigh I asked the duke what he was doing so far from his palace
at this hour
Smirking, he wondered what I was doing away from my own palace at
this time
My eyes were piercing daggers as I pushed my way past him, not at all
gently
With a strong hand on my arm, he stopped my retreat and pulled me
closer
Looking much more uncertain than I had ever seen him, he met my
sharp stare
Asking if I would allow him to accompany me back, for dusk was on its
way

It was then I wondered why he had halted his horse so quickly, so insistently
Possibly so he could be near me as soon as possible, out of worry, out of care
As he waited anxiously for my response, some of my irritation melted away
I let him lead me to where his mare was waiting, and he effortlessly lifted me
He set me carefully atop the saddle, then jumped up and settled in behind me

On our long sunset journey, our conversation flowed easily, to my surprise
He listened to every word from my mouth with such rapt, spellbound attention
With his warm chest against my back, I could have sworn I heard his heartbeat
The organ fiercely thumping under his skin, longing to be closer to my own heart

Suddenly, it was hard to imagine that we were normally at such tense odds
I began to lament over the upsetting fact that our trip was almost complete
And for the first time in years, I began thinking of that all-consuming love
Wondering if maybe, it was not as far out of reach as I had once imagined

Candlelit Window

Run toward the gilded gates of the castle that graciously and swiftly
open for you
Feel the abundance of rose bushes prick your skin as you continue your
journey
Let the pelting droplets of rain from the storm wash away the burgeon-
ing blood
Keep your eyes fixed on the window with the tall candlesticks glowing
on the sill
Hope that the flickering light means your love is awake still, waiting for
you to come
Feel the fierce wind whip at your back; hear the untamed thunder trail-
ing after you
Pick up the smallest of stones, harmless enough to cast up to her closed
window
Closer now; get ready to toss one of the rocks high above to signal your
presence
Then realize there is no need, for her silhouette is revealed by a flash of
lightning

There she stands, opening her window to call down to you, beckoning
you to come up
Filled with elation, begin to climb the vines of ivy plastered all along the
castle walls
Finally reach your love; feel her doting hand caress your cheek, warming
you instantly
Assure her that there is no circumstance, no storm or siege, that could
keep you apart
Crawl through the tall window and wrap her in your arms—a tight and
tender embrace
Blow out the golden candle, for there is no need for the dim flames to
continue burning
Not when you and your love are back together again, reunited against
all odds
Ever so grateful that the cloak of night can cover you both in darkness
From the heavy burdens and troubles that the light of day will forever
bring

Jealousy

Lady of the court, dressed in a sultry gossamer gown crafted from golden silk
Suitors surrounded me instantly, eagerly, while you were nowhere to be found
Later you spotted me twirling in the arms of another across the ballroom
Instantly a look of fury was written upon your domineering, enraged face
Perhaps if you had desired so strongly to be the one whose body I held onto
You should have said so; you should have whispered it to me under the stars
Even still, as I was pressed against another who admired me so openly
My body would not move for this man the way it always moved for you
Though his arms tensed around me, my hips moved to the beat of my heart
A besotted heart that, begrudgingly, I knew would only beat for you
I longed for you to sweep me off my feet, to pry his greedy hands from my waist
Please, let me show you what my body can do if you tell me you still want me
Plucking my thoughts from my mind, you stalked over to me with determination
Pushing the other man aside as if he were no more than a fly, you led me away
A murderous glint shone in your deep green eyes as I felt your gaze in my bones
Spreading through my body like a thunderstorm, the feeling transfixing, gripping
Your rough voice was full of rasp as you spoke into my ear, murmuring,
Your heart is mine, just as your body is mine, for no one else is worthy of you
Stomach fluttering, I melted into your touch, relieved to be back in your arms
Though I wished it did not take the sight of me with another to get me here

Coronation

With her royal coronation only hours away
The future queen began carefully dressing
Gently gliding the ball gown down her body
Feeling the gauzy fabric hugging her curves
A true red shade embellished the regal dress
Intertwined with excessive golden threads
Ribbons featured in the back tied so securely
She knew deep imprints would be left behind
A reminder of the permanence of this night

The gown displayed an indecently deep neckline
Leading down to a forcefully cinched waistline
Cascading from her curved hips to the ground
Puddling against the crystalline marble floors
As she glided down the winding staircase
The dress effortlessly moved along with her
Pirouetting as if it had become animated
Swaying from the breeze in the castle's air

As she entered the imperial throne room
A hush instantly fell upon the crowd
But the queen paid them no mind at all
For her eyes were cemented elsewhere
To the crown—*her crown*—awaiting her

Jasmine flowers were carefully arranged
Between the gems embedded in place
The dainty white petals a stark contrast
To the shimmering, otherworldly jewels
The black opals and crystal diamonds
Set within the rare and regal headpiece

The crown was never promised to her
Though she knew it would fit perfectly
She fought every day to earn this title
And now she would fight to keep it
The realm did not need a king to save
It needed an exceptional queen to rule
The crown was placed upon her head
And the room began to bow before her
Humbly whispering to their new ruler
Quiet chants of *long live the queen*

Origin of Villains

Villains do not enter this world with hatred in their hearts, for evil is created
Wickedness catches them, like a heartless demon lurking within the darkness
Hidden in the shadows, searching for anyone willing to hand over their soul
Desperate enough to let their humanity be replaced by a pit of dark oblivion

Villains know and see all, with eyes concealing a cold, calculating clarity
They will hide in plain sight, roaming the halls of castles, befriending royalty
Taking note of every pernicious response and each spiteful look hurled their way
Then they will start to strategize, scheme, salivate for the taste of vengeance

Say what you will about cruel villains, but do not dare to doubt their dedication
Revenge requires a slow-moving, yet exact, degree of patience and persistence
With abandoned morals spilled on the floor like a broken string of ivory pearls
And incensed with contempt, villains take that anger brimming inside of them
And use it as fuel to bide their time, waiting for the right moment to strike

When their hands are tarnished with bloodshed and their enemies have fallen
They will look within and realize that without that dense burden of retribution
Their heart does not know how to keep beating, for it has purpose no longer
And they will crumble to the merciless floor just as their enemies once did

Masquerade

The masquerade was held under the moonlight of a cool spring night, secrets littering the air
Intricate masks rested upon the stoic faces of regal guests, keen to obscure their identities
Though their nefarious mentalities would filter through and reveal themselves, mask or not
One mask stood out among the rest, bejeweled with more gems than anyone could wish for
Resplendent rubies, sapphires of the deepest blues, enchanting emeralds, all placed with care
Glistening greater than any star in the sky, it was a wonder anyone was able to look elsewhere
The mask was stunning, yet the woman wearing it was a greater sight than any jewel in existence

Men and women alike tried to steal her notice, needing to exist in her orbit if just for one night
The woman of unmatched beauty did not long for their admiration, though she earned it even so
She wished only to admire the moon, bathe in the ethereal sparkle, then slip away without notice
Still, without opening her mouth, without speaking the words in her mind, people gaped at her
Fireflies dotingly lingered around her, and nightingales excitedly followed her every step
Trees swayed in her direction as if even nature could not deny the energy of her magnetism

A man clad in a simple, modest mask was among those who were instantly enamored by her
Though he did not notice her decorative mask, her crimson lips, or her chiffon-covered body
Instead he felt her soul speaking softly to his, and he found his feet moving, walking toward her
As if the stars could not sleep until he knew what it felt like to be seen by her, at least once

She felt him before she saw him, and for the only time that night, for
the only time in her life
The alluring woman understood what others felt when they confessed
they were drawn to her
The man did not stop until he stood so close that she had to tilt her
head back to meet his eyes
Barely visible through the mask yet capable of boring into hers with the
ferocity of a wildfire
His stare penetrated deep within her bones, and still, she did not flinch
away from his attention

Instead she leaned into him even further, while steadily placing her
hand upon his strong chest
Meeting his gaze with the same intensity, though her eyes revealed a
sincere and gentle nature
One that nearly sank him to his knees, and it was then he knew that she
was his, as he was hers

A kingdom of suitors yearned for her, but it was a yearning that could
never be reciprocated
For it was written so clearly in the fabric of the cosmos that these two
belonged together
Though it was a tragedy that others could not see the way his thoughts
echoed her own
And her soul sang only for him, just as his sang only for her, until all
others were forgotten

When they whispered their names to each other, the sky wept at the
sight of this fond moment
Even the constellations above knew with complete certainty and clarity
that this was true love
And it was blooming right before their dampened eyes, in the midst of
the moonlit masquerade

Sapphire Prince

As a quiet handmaiden, I felt as invisible as a ghost within the enormity of the daunting palace
I spent my days silently roaming the wide halls and sometimes wondered if I really was a ghost
If I tragically perished and simply was not made aware of it, for no one bothered to tell me
Royals would frequently dart across the many halls: powerful queens, less powerful kings
Cavalier and careless princes, elegant and exquisite princesses, all well known, all adored
And yet I continued to remain unseen for what felt like a never-ending eternity

Long after dusk, as I read by fading candlelight in the library, I felt a gaze settle upon me
Rare as it was, it felt like being struck by lightning: jolting, yet invigorating all the same
I knew him to be a prince though he carried no sense of arrogance, only intoxicating charm
I have seen you before, the prince abruptly spoke, his voice low and rough and almost improper
In a daze, I knew the potent cadence of his voice would linger in my head long after he left
I do not think so, for I would have remembered the attention of one such as yourself, I replied
I spoke meekly, worried he might simply vanish from my sight if my voice grew too loud
Ah, that is why I know I have seen you, for I remember pining for your notice after one glance
He replied with a smirk while I looked down, breathless, pretending to be immersed in my book
But not before catching a glimpse of his piercing eyes, as blue as any ocean I had ever seen

Well, all you needed was to ask, and I would have granted it, I answered,
my blush deepening
*I am glad, for now that I have your attention, I intend to hold it captive, if
you will have me*
The prince said while moving closer, lightly grazing my arm as he came
to sit beside me

*I am not sure why I have interested you, for I am as notable as a speck of
dust on the castle walls*
And you seem to be as illuminating as all the stars within the sky, I bashful-
ly answered, blushing
*Oh, but if I am a star, then you are the moon: more pearlescent than I could
ever dream of being*
*You are radiant, and if people are blind to that, it is only because they have
never dared to look*
Or perhaps your light is too much for them to bear, he then whispered,
with complete reverence

With clear yearning in his sapphire eyes, he tentatively moved his hand
toward my own
When I did not protest—when I looked up at him imploringly—he
intertwined our fingers
Softly touching me as if I were made of glass and he was terrified I
would soon shatter
He moved closer, and when there was no space left between us at all,
my heart sped up
It then dawned on me that I must truly be alive—fully living—neither
a ghost nor a spirit
With a rare smile on my lips and a hopeful look in my eyes, I leaned
into his warm touch
And felt as though after tonight, my days in the castle would no longer
feel dismal at all

Ecstasy of Excitement

The palace seemed to be the most alive right before a ball
Marble floors hungered to be danced upon into the night
Bare walls delighted in being strewn with vibrant decor
Lanterns were lit, and flames grew with a burning passion
Appetizers were prepared: delectable morsels to feast upon
Towering cakes with mouthwatering buttercream and berries
Glasses of effervescent champagne floated around the room
Urging all to indulge in the dizzying flavor of the clear wine
Music filled with percussion soon reverberated off the walls
Chandeliers of a thousand crystals began to sway to the beat
Royal guests conversed spiritedly, glad to unwind for a night
The ground soon began to shake, for the dancing did not relent
Did not stop until blood coated the interior of elegant high heels
Heiresses marveled at the luxurious gowns flaunted around
Flowing fabrics in hues of striking silvers and midnight blues
Luxurious dresses ornamented with rare, glittering gemstones
Elongated, sleek gloves adorned outstretched, graceful arms
Stolen glances and ephemeral touches ensued through the night
Even the most deceitful thieves and cheats found a way inside
As the palace would not deny a single soul from the revelry
For it savored the ecstasy of excitement far too much

Someone New

Dance after dance, her feet began to ache, her patience began to thin
She was growing faint from the suffocating sense of dreariness in the air
Though the imperial ballroom was undoubtedly magnificent and glorious
The same could not be said about its grim guests and mundane suitors
With every hour that passed, she graciously indulged her many admirers
Each one was entirely besotted, and she was simply uninterested in
them all

It was not until she felt a new, enthralling presence make himself known
That she began to perk up, instantly ever so curious of who he might be
She felt his eyes on her from across the ballroom, burning holes into her
back
Realizing—as she slowly turned—that she had underestimated the
hunger
Written clearly on his face, seeping from his body and wafting toward
her
Her feet began to move determinedly of their own transfixed volition
She felt his wolflike aura—full of power and cunning—descend upon
her
Drawn to him, she moved quicker, only to find him now inches away
Leaning up against the wall, assertively, she risked a glance at his face
And was pleased to find that the intensity in his gaze had only deepened
His face was colored by unabashed craving as if only she could satiate
him
If he had asked to drink from her, to feed from her warm, inviting neck
She would have obliged, engrossed in the way he continued to stare
Looking at her in a way no one else at the ball had ventured to

Though he did not ask for those things; he merely stepped closer
Reaching his hand up, which was almost trembling with desire
He slowly began to trace the outline of her lips with his fingers
And rasped in a surprisingly low and steady voice, *come with me*
She let this enigma of a man possessively lead her out of the room
Guiding the way to her doom or her freedom, she was not yet sure
Though her body was humming with a tempting need to find out

Haunted Castle

The haunted atmosphere within the rustic castle starts to seep into the
ballroom
The once indulgent and gentle music coming from the piano begins to
crescendo
Entering into a chillingly eerie minor key, seeming to summon all that
is evil
The guests regard the music as a thorn on their skin—one they cannot
pluck out
Discreet whispers turn into hurried, concerned remarks, while lights
now crackle
As if to warn of an ominous, impending presence bringing certain
disaster to all

Just outside, the thrashing wind picks up, and the grand, oak doors
suddenly slam shut
The guests glance around, perceiving their own fear mirrored in the
wary eyes of others
Music starts to pick up in tempo, faster, as if the keys cannot be played
quick enough
To convey the calamity that has flooded into the room like an unsus-
pecting, silent spirit
Candles are blown out as quickly as they are lit; windows shatter in
seamless unison
Guests strain their voices to hear each other, for the chaos and destruc-
tion is deafening
Though the terror in their eyes is enough to express the message of
panic and horror

The pianist is lost to the evil of the night, unable to stop playing his
unnerving tune
Invisible hands are punitively placed over his trembling ones, urging
him to continue
Inevitably the chandelier falls, teardrop crystals flying through the air
like shooting stars
The ballroom is encased in pitch black, and the guests fall to the floor,
one after another
The sinister entity moving quickly, vindictively, to soundlessly bring
them all to their feet

As the last guest falls, their eyes vacant, their hair spread beneath them
like a golden river
The piano descends into a familiar, memorable tune once again: a me-
lodic, ethereal song
Though the pianist now plays with a grim undertone, distraught from
all that has happened
The lights spark and then shine back to life, casting dim light upon the
sea of lifeless bodies
Eventually the music ends, and the exhausted pianist collapses to the
floor beside the guests
The haunted aura slinks out of the ballroom, grateful that the castle is
once again quiet

Envelope of Wanting

The king longed dreadfully for a queen he could not have
Rivalries waged on within the kingdoms that divided them
The queen loved the king silently, so sure they could never be
Until one morning a letter arrived, sealed with a blood-red stamp
The scarlet wax had dripped down the front of the sealed envelope
As if the writer could not wait another moment before sending it off

The queen opened the letter with trembling fingers
Knowing without seeing a single word who wrote it for her
She could feel the presence of the king merely by holding his note
Hope building in her throat, she carefully read every word

The king had poured out the contents of his whole heart to the queen
Telling her that every night he dreamed only of her—of her voice
Revealing that he would give up his title, his nation, his crown
If it meant they had a chance to be together, if she felt the same
The queen, tears streaming down her face, gasped at these words
Of course she felt the same and was sure that she eternally would

Her handmaiden asked if the queen wished to write a letter in reply
But the infatuated ruler was already running to the royal carriages
Determined to deliver her response to her king—her love—in person
To put aside the obligation of her crown and take his hand in hers
Promising to never let their gilded thrones come between them again

Baroque Dagger

She looked at him reverentially, a small smile blossoming when he
turned to face her
When she saw what he held, though, her face instantly cracked like an
unlucky mirror
The baroque dagger in his hand felt lighter than the weight of what he
was about to do
Knuckles turning white from gripping the blade, too exquisite to be
used for destruction
The tip of the dagger dragged a languid path along her skin, slowly and
deliberately so
Igniting a medley goosebumps in its wake, until her mind raced with
inescapable fear

She thought she saw regret in his eyes, a sense of guilt surrounding his
sudden betrayal
But her eyes were misty with the threat of tears, and once she blinked
them all away
She realized she was mistaken, for there was no shame hidden in his
darkening gaze
Only an assured sense of obligation, knowing that only he could be the
one to do this
She did not fault him for his steady resolve; it was something she ad-
mired, even envied
Although just this once she wished his hand would have a slight, yet
noticeable, tremor
That his chest would rise and fall rapidly, that his eyes would shed even
one tear for her

Though none of that came to be, and he simply traced his free hand
along her neck
Slowly moving to cup her face, touching her skin with such sensitive,
subtle adoration
That if his other hand had not moved to deeply plunge the dagger into
her chest
She might have felt as though they were simply in a lover's embrace, full
of passion

Looking on with muted horror, he dragged the blade through her flesh, slicing her open
Her blood spilled out like wine, as if an expensive merlot had filled her veins all along
And she had been mistaken before, but now, as her eyes fought a permanent slumber
She was sure she saw a flash of something akin to true love and deep, horrific remorse
Passing through his eyes like a meteor shower, so bright and mesmerizing in the moment
Yet when it passes, all you are left with is a dark and empty sky, leaving you with longing

As that warm light in his eyes departed too soon, her own eyes gave way to total darkness
Though she was at least relieved that her last, dying sight had been the soft look in his eyes
A look that betrayed his actions and granted her a soft sense of peace before drifting away
She knew that although his betrayal cut deep, once the knife of treachery had been dislodged
Her lover's truth had spilled free like fallen ink, revealing everything she needed to know

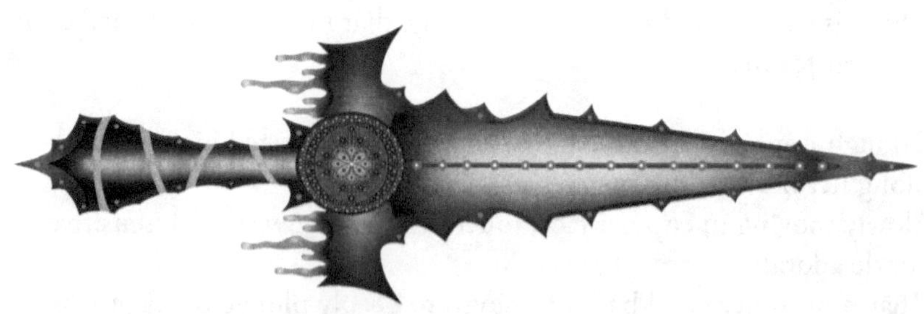

Mask of Certainty

My crown weighed heavily upon my thick and glossy chestnut hair
I did not know what hurt more, the crown, or the burden of my duty
The rubies and sapphires dug into my scalp, I was dizzy with nerves
Though I raged and ached deep within, my feet did not once stumble
My voice remained steady and assertive, and my steely stare persisted
As I addressed the room, speaking words full of false hope, forced ease
I spoke of a future I did not believe in, of a land I did not want to lead

When conversations resumed, and lively music filtered into the room
I drifted over to a peaceful, abandoned corner of the now bustling room
A gentle hand on my shoulder alerted me of his presence until I turned
At once, I felt inclined to resent him as my mask of certainty collapsed
How could someone so unfamiliar, so unknown, affect me this instantly
Boldly, he reached for my crown, and before I had a chance to protest
He wordlessly removed it from my hair and placed it beside me with care
Without sparing the opulent jewels a second glance, his eyes fixed on mine
Instead he smoothed my flowing hair, tucking the strands behind my ears
And by way of a miracle, my mind felt clearer than it had all night long

I asked *why*, and for an intimate moment, he gazed deeply into my wide eyes
Only to then roam across my face, as if he wanted to memorize my every feature
At last he replied, *it looked agonizing, and I could not bear to see you in any pain*
It hurt me just as it was hurting you, and I ached as if it was upon my own head
Stunned by the sincerity in his voice, I silently urged him away from the party
Into the calm evening air, away from all others, where we could breathe easier
And as our eyes locked once more, we inhaled steadily and finally felt relief

Forever Caged

Held captive in a castle dungeon, in a cage, chains clasped to my hands
year after year
The enclosure was constructed with genuine silver, decorated with spell-
binding jewels
Every inch was incessantly shining until it was difficult to tell that it was
a cage at all

Yet, I still felt bound, forcefully confined to such a narrow space, forget-
ting life above
No longer could I picture the pale moon up in the sky or the green
grass upon the ground
The only thing that touched me now were these cuffs on my wrists, cold
and threatening

One day, I found the courage to carefully bring my hand up to one of
the glossy bars
But the slightest touch pricked my finger, for the points of the gems
were sharpened spikes
As I watched the blood create a small rivulet of crimson, running down
my wounded hand
I felt more hopeless than ever before, sure that these walls were watch-
ing me slowly die

Time passed by as my chains grew tighter, a cruel and constant remind-
er of my captivity
With every royal festivity I heard taking place above, every laugh ring-
ing through the halls
I wondered if they knew there was such depravity occurring within the
dungeons down below
If they ever heard my endless shouting, each shriek scraping my throat
raw with the effort

But as years passed, I was helped by none and seen by none, only fated to this grim isolation
Though what I had done to deserve this solitary sentence of desolation, none would ever know
Maybe someday they will free me, unshackle my hands, allow me to feel the sun on my skin
Until then, I will remain in this cage of gems, and as the bars gleam, my own light will dim
And soon I will be filled with nothing but bleak darkness, and there will be no one to notice

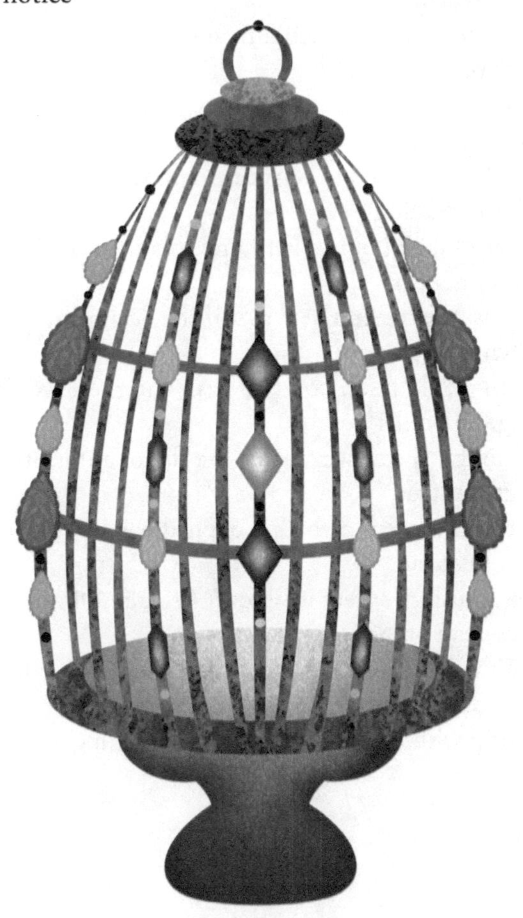

Runaway Bride

The royal wedding was about to begin, yet the queen had no intentions of reciting her vows
It was not that her betrothed was wicked in any sense; he was merely not who her heart desired
In fact her heart only longed to be freed from this majestic life, to live in quiet simplicity
The prosperity of a nation on her shoulders was too much to bear, as was the idea of this union
Outfitted in a glorious gown crafted from white lace, the queen felt sickeningly overwhelmed
She thought of escaping to the countryside surrounded by green hills and vast flower patches
Never again would she have to rule, dole out punishments, or make plans for war after war
Her life would be dedicated to plucking berries from bushes, dreamily baking, and lazily reading
Though she was snapped out of her fantasy as the bridal procession began to echo in her ears
Feeling nauseous, the queen knew that if she decided to go through with this unifying ceremony
Then her dream would never come to pass, and there would be no berries, no baking, no books
She would be resigned to a wearisome life full of authority and responsibility she never wanted
As the doors to the ancient cathedral opened before her and she spotted her soon-to-be husband
The queen felt a rush of surety wash over her trembling body, and though all eyes were on her
She picked up the skirts of her heavy, tulle-laden dress, and began to run toward the countryside
Heart drumming with excitement and eyes sparkling with mirth the whole journey there

Sinfully Yours

My decadently depraved love,

I write this letter to you, my villain who loves as urgently as he fights
Though you march onto the battlefield with ruin running through you
A wicked gleam in your eyes at the thought of damage and destruction
Know that I feel your sweet love even in those moments of mayhem
Remember that I am yours in this life, just as I will be yours in death
No more than a grieving ghost, morosely haunting until you join me
Your many opponents are right to fear you, to recoil from your scorn
But they are not aware of the empathy that lies beneath the malevolence
They do not know that your ruthless hands are often exceedingly gentle
That your hoarse voice becomes timid only when you talk to me of love
Beneath the singed coating of your darkened heart lies such warmth
Sometimes, late at night, when the air is still, I can almost hear you
Whispering the softest words of tender devotion upon my bare skin
I can almost hear your heart beating just beneath your chest, for me
Hopefully you can hear my heart pounding longingly for you too
I beg you to read my loving prose and feel me with you, beside you
Hold onto this letter until the day that you can once again hold me

Sinfully yours, for as long as we have together, and beyond

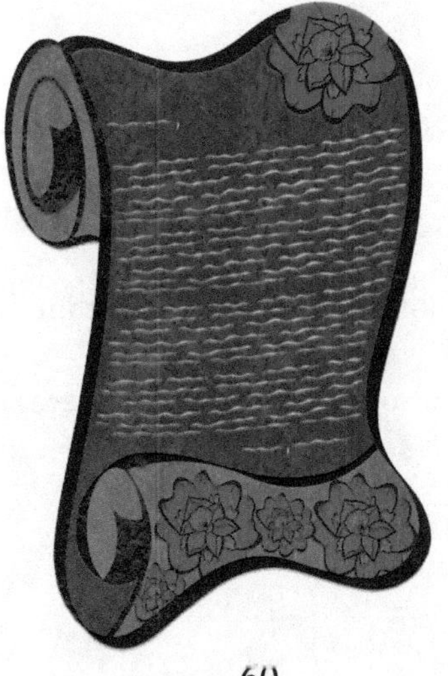

Eager to Dream

The ballroom was bustling with waltzing couples letting the music guide their movements
I roamed toward the large wooden doors, engraved with tales of royals who came before us
Letting my gown trail behind me like a sapphire puddle, creating small waves with each step
As I reached the small sanctuary of a deserted balcony, I felt a firm hand grasp at my elbow
Pulling me back until I was flush against this stranger, or so I believed him to be a stranger

In the very back of my mind, I felt a strange, yet persistent sense of familiarity with him
The way you feel when flowers start to bloom in the spring, for you have seen them before
And yet each season brings new excitement at the blossom's reemergence in your garden
The man looked down at me, searching my face for any hesitation, any discomfort, any fear
When he seemingly found none, he pressed me closer to him, which was almost impossible
Though entirely welcome, for he felt so calming against me, like shelter during a rainstorm

I began to ask if we knew each other, though it seemed clear I *would have* remembered him
But the words I had been searching for died upon my tongue when he suddenly reached out
And captured my rosy bottom lip between his thumb and forefinger, stroking ever so gently
He looked upon me as if some secret had been revealed, just by gazing deeply into my eyes

Letting out a sharp breath, full of wanting, he dropped his hand and backed away, only a step

The absence of his body against mine left me vexingly cold on this hot summer evening

Looking at me one last time before walking away, he smirked knowingly and affectionately

A sight I would think of for days to come, and whispered to me, *I will see you in your dreams*

And ss he left, suddenly I could not wait for the night to be over, so I could drift off into sleep

Duel

A duel was declared in which two men would fight for the honor of her love
Real love, she wearily thought, *should neither begin nor end with such bloodshed*
How could she learn to trust their touch when their hands hold such violence
The men were prepared to duel to the death, to gallantly lay down their lives
If it meant they had a chance to win her love—love that she had never offered
The sky turned murky and violent, rain clouds heavy with an ominous warning
She watched in palpable horror, thinking that if no one listened to her pleas now
Then what sort of life would she look forward to with one of these foolish men?
She did not wish to be loved as an unseen ghost would be, certain to be ignored
The men stepped forward, guns drawn, fingers on the trigger, death in the air
She stepped between the two just as the sound of gunfire echoed in their ears
They gazed at her with horror in their eyes, shock etched into their expressions
As her ruddy blood flowed out, she felt satisfied that she chose her own ending
For any other outcome would have condemned her to a different sort of death
A slower demise at the hands of a man she could not love, not today, not ever

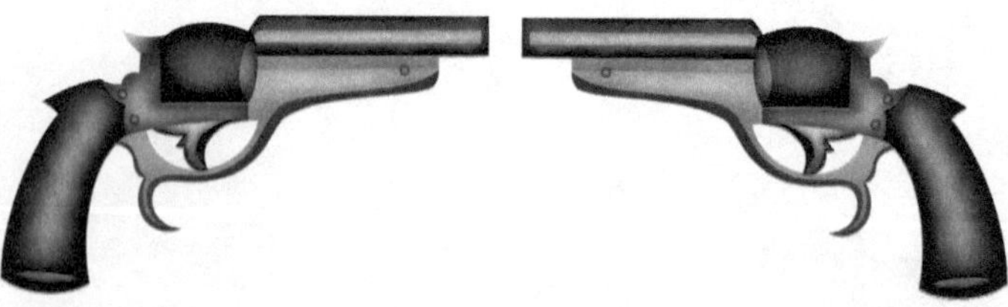

Russian Rescue

The unforgiving chill of Russia made my gloved hands tremble
I longed for a warm, crackling fire and a cup of hot, steaming tea
Hastily I continued walking along the bustling cobblestone streets
When a strong hand wrapped around my waist, pulling me back
Their other hand pressing sternly over my now screaming mouth
My captor held me so close, his dark, wavy hair falling into my face
The scent of leather and suede momentarily stunned me into a daze
Snapping out of it, I knew I was in grave danger being away in this alley
As grand duchess of Russia, I was always ordered to be guarded
Though this night I had wandered off, wishing for time to myself
Now I longed for the familiar security and strength my sentries brought

Resisting relentlessly, my captor pinned me with a look of exasperation
In a thick, deep accent he quietly rushed out that I was being followed
By loathsome men who sought to abduct me for their own nefarious
gain
My ransom was to be presented to the royals, an insurmountable sum
Though it was not certain that these thieves would elect to spare my life
Even if they were gifted all of the gold and gems the palace had to offer
I looked at this man still holding onto me with narrowed, unsure eyes
Wildly irritated at my reluctance to believe him, he slightly stepped
back
Letting me go, holding up his hardened hands to show he meant no
harm
Temporarily placated, I followed his covert gaze now eyeing the street
There were indeed men with malice on their faces storming toward us
Locking eyes with the man who warned me, we both knew what to do
As he promptly intertwined our hands, and without hesitation, we ran

Gothic Manor

Built on a hilltop, beside a neglected cemetery, sat a gothic manor
The austere fortress had been first constructed many centuries ago
Though it remained hauntingly magnificent after all these years
With its pointed arches, baroque detailing, and mosaic lined walls
It was beautifully sinister, yet no one would risk venturing inside
For the manor possessed an air of something wicked living within
So the cautious town below decided it best to admire from afar

In truth, while howling crows and the aura of death circled the home
One lone man lived inside, and he was far from a creature or spirit
He simply yearned for a long life of eerie adventure and excitement
And it was this absence of such thrills that continued to plague him so
The manor, though decidedly menacing by its morose outward façade
Did not dispense the sense of mystery he had spent his life craving

The forlorn man hoped something evil would emerge from the dark
Find its way into the manor, and head straight for his blunted heart
But no such luck had come to pass, though he waited and waited
His days roaming the manor's wide halls remained as mundane as ever
Often, he spoke to the sky while gazing out his ornately hewn windows
Asking for something electrifying and unknown to come to his door
And when the dissonant, booming sound of his grand doorbell rang out
He sprinted with impatience to see what sort of corruption awaited him
For the cosmos he had begged to for all those years had finally listened

Wounded

As I stumbled into the palace in darkness, the hemorrhaging of my wounds would not relent
Intent on bathing the rubies sewed into the satin material of my gown in such stark, bloody gore
My eyes were inflamed from an onslaught of tears, and my throat was hoarse from screaming
Thick blood worked its way up and up until a steady stream flowed from my parted mouth
Yet I still searched for you, tried to call your name, but all that came out was a whisper
And though my ragged voice was near silent, you still emerged from the shadows of the night
With worry etched on your face, as if you could sense something had gone horribly wrong
Overcome with elation at your presence, I frantically tried to stumble into your inviting arms
Attempting to close the excruciating distance between us, staggering more with every step

Suddenly you were right in front of me and I could see the pool of unshed tears lining your eyes
You held my waist securely in your shaking hands and took in the abundance of my injuries
My swollen, split lip, stung from the sharp breeze blowing in from the open palace doors
The discolored bruises covering my arms and throat, already a collage of the deepest purples
The lengthy gash in my stomach, suddenly spilling less blood than when I first arrived
And I realized, as you were gripping my waist, you were also putting pressure on my wound
Steering me away from my impending doom, as if you would challenge death himself to save me

You grabbed my wrist, your hold firm but tender enough to cease my trembling for a moment
Looking up, I gazed into your eyes, which held nothing but obvious worry and unshakable love
I let you bandage my wounds with a devoted focus, your brows drawn close in concentration
Knowing you could not fathom stopping until all my injuries were hidden under gauze
Until you could peel my bloodied dress from my body, wash away any specks of scarlet
And as you picked me up, ever so dotingly, and carried me in your arms so I could finally rest
I knew I would be able to sleep easily with you right beside me as the memory of tonight faded
For you made sure that any trace of my anguish had been thoroughly extinguished
Blown away like ash in the unforgiving wind, unable to wound me for one moment longer

Lovesick Knight

The maiden was banished, exiled, thrown out into the cold
Crawling away from the palace, she wept with such woe
The sweet girl found refuge deep within the farthest forest
Where she wore bunches of flower petals upon her soft skin
Hoping to blend into the woods, so no trouble would find her
She spent her days softly singing to small woodland creatures
And her nights lounging by the surrounding babbling brooks
Watching the water bask in the incandescence of the stars

The lovesick knight had hopelessly fallen for the fair maiden
When she left, he felt empty, as bereaved as a lonely widow
He set off immediately, refusing to rest until she was found
She helped him breathe a little easier in such a troubled world
The maiden was his salvation, and he hoped he was hers as well
As he searched he never lost hope; his heart would not allow it
Then, mercifully, he felt her divine presence within his reach
He knew that she was behind him without even turning around
And yet he did; needing to look upon her as she ran into his arms
He checked her skin relentlessly for wounds and sores and cuts
And when she assured him that she was entirely unharmed
He wept with stark relief, with undiluted love and adoration

Reunited, the forest floor pulled the maiden down to the ground
As if her knees belonged in the mud, her hands belonged in the dirt
Where she could gaze up at her knight and pray to him endlessly
She would stay on the ground day and night if it meant he would stay
Yet he quickly fell to the ground as well, taking her face in his hands
Never wanting her lovely neck to ache, never wanting her eyes to strain
He should be the one on his knees, for she is his goddess, his perfect
deity

With love in her eyes, she whispered, *I did not know if you would come
for me*
With lovestruck devotion written on every line of his face, he tenderly
spoke
In the darkest of nights, even the faraway moon would guide me back to you
With that, the knight and his love laid their bodies down upon the lush
soil
Surrounded by woodland creatures and forest flowers, they now felt
grateful
For the maiden's exile had led them both to where they truly needed to
be
Among the woods, that would shelter their precious love until the end
of time

The Cliff

The enemies sprinted through the forest, dimly lit only by the distant glow of the moon
Bundles of twigs snapped beneath their hurried feet like a cacophony of breaking bones
The air smelled of pine needles and moss, and wolves howled with menacing premonition
The palpable hatred brimming within the rivals urged their legs to move faster and faster
The villain was a breath away from the hero, so close he could see the sweat lining his neck
Which was more distracting than he had ever anticipated, and yet, they both continued on

Running deeper into the woods until the hero looked back and saw nothing but darkness
Thinking he had outrun his rival, he halted, out of breath, though he had stopped far too fast
The ground seemed to move under him, propelling the hero farther and farther across the dirt
Until all at once he began to fall over a cliff, so fast the villain could scarcely process the sight
At the last moment, the villain flung out an arm and reached frantically out for his rival
Just barely did he grasp onto the hero's hand, which was trembling, gripping the forest floor

Their eyes connected, the villain's light blue eyes ready to burst with blatant, profound panic
The hero's deep green eyes erupted with the terrifying disbelief that followed a brush with death
Lifting the hero into his arms, the villain did not let go until they were stable, on solid ground

The hero did not need to ask why the villain saved him when they had
always seemed at odds
For the question was already lingering between them in a way that
could no longer be ignored
The villain deepened his grip around the hero, afraid to break their
connection, and shyly spoke
*This world will never be worth destroying if you are not in it to try and stop
me at every turn*

Stunned, the hero allowed himself to gaze upon the villain with a fleet-
ing sense of admiration
Before leaning forward, swiftly pushing his foe off the cliff, and watch-
ing as he fell to his death
Standing and brushing the dust and soil off his now ragged attire, the
hero silently walked away
The only witnesses to his true nature were the verdant trees, the cold
dirt, and the silver moon
And with no remorse, he was certain they would all keep his sinister
secret until the end of time

End of an Era

The gothic, medieval crown suddenly fell from the queen's burgundy
hair
As her body began to submit to the biting acidity coating her lips and
lungs
The queen knew she did not have much longer, for she had been de-
ceived
To be in a position of royal power always comes with the most deadly of
risks
So many longed to take her throne for themselves, to bask in imperial
control
Though now the queen did not give any thought to the identity of her
traitor
She only wished that her love would return to her before she met her
demise

Her thoughts were only of him: his eyes, his voice, his touch, his love
for her
The queen had written him a letter, which now sat unfinished upon her
desk
But she worried the words would not convey everything he meant to
her
She wished she could craft him a constellation, a gleaming gift in the
sky
Each star proving the enormity of her infatuated love, of her loyal
affection

The poison was now moving quickly, too quickly, through her blood-
stream
The rosy hue of her once blushing cheeks grew dull beneath her pallid
skin
Her sage green eyes drained of their color until nothing but a void
remained
All of a sudden her love darted in, rushing right to her side, panting
with fear
Now her color should rush back and her body should grow as warm as
a furnace

For the strength of their love—his mere presence—would drive the poison away
But even together, with their hands tightly interlaced, neither wanting to let go
It was not enough, for the queen's face suddenly froze, unmoving with death
And her love watched in devastated horror as she remained cold and desolate
The toxins in her veins had burnt out the regal, resolute fire within her blood
And not even an unfailing love such as theirs could reignite the fallen queen

Part 1001: Fantasy

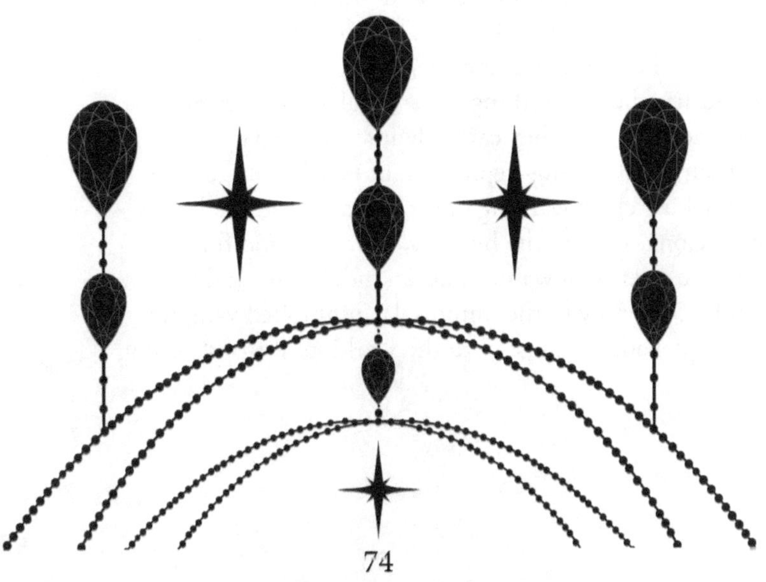

Vampiric Love

Vampires love one another so freely and so often
For they are not bound by the fickle confines of time
They are not troubled with the dark shadow of mortality
A ticking clock clouding their minds, ruling their hearts
For a while their love and adoration bloom like a rose
Blossoming in the early, sun-kissed days of springtime
Excessive in their affections, uninhibited in their desires
Yet even vampires are not immune to the voice of envy
Whispering spiteful words full of bitterness into their ears
Lifetimes pass by speedily and soundlessly as ever before
And these undying beings become jealous of mere mortals
Because they realize that, given the fragility of an earthly life
Never promised, continuously capable of being cut short
Mortals must make the power of their love that much greater
It must seem as urgent as rainclouds nearing a wildfire
For they must love with the fervor of a flickering flame
A fire that is on the verge of being extinguished too soon
Eternal vampires will never understand this crucial need
To touch, to kiss, to caress as if it may be their last time
For their undead lovers will always draw another breath
They will live to see a new day, walk this world once more
And as these sour reminders weigh upon their cold hearts
They will then turn and find their lover smiling at them
And realize there is nothing bitter at all about this fate
Not when it means they can fully lose themselves in love
Without the daunting trepidation of ever having to stop
That ticking clock warning of such fatality and finality
That belongs only to the humans, so mortal and fragile
And an existence of wanton, never-ending love and lust
That belongs only to the immortal, uninhibited vampires
Who will gladly indulge until the world itself stops turning

Witchcraft

Witchcraft was birthed atop the jade wings of a spiraling dragonfly
An incantation had fallen upon a seed stuck beneath the warm earth
Growing, blossoming, until a small enchanted flower soon emerged
All those who ventured to touch the charmed petals were thus spelled
To feel a blazing spark inflame and detonate deep within their souls
Hence magic engulfed them at once and the first witches came to be
Enchantments were passionately spoken aloud in garden after garden
Until none could resist the magic wafting off these bewitched flowers
Witches were born in abundance, then traveled as one to a new land
A secluded land they called their own, known as the Witch Kingdom
This came to be the only land that men would never scheme to invade
These women—the witches—held more power within their fingertips
Than the men could ever find within the sharp points of their weapons
Witchcraft flowed through their blood, ageless with infinite knowledge
Their power protected the land, ensuring it would forever guard them
They seized their magic straight from the soft petals of prickly plants
Swearing never to return the mesmerizing flowers back to the ground
Magic grew on this land, as incantations were whispered into the air
The charms soared and sailed across clouds until found by a dragonfly
And the spell settled easily onto its wings, beginning the cycle anew

Infatuated Devil

Though he was meant to reside in hell, side by side with the demons
The Devil ventured to Earth, and as all love stories go, he fell deeply
The fact that she was a mortal agonized the Devil from dawn to dusk
In time, the mortal loved him back; how could she resist his rapt notice
How could she deny the effect he had on her as he smiled his wry smile
In hell the Devil was uncaring, merciless, yielding to the will of none
But with his mortal he counted her eyelashes when she slept beside him
He rubbed his hands up and down her arms the moment she grew cold
The Devil, monster of the darkness, harbinger of death, loved his mortal
As tenderly as a ladybug might land upon one's finger on a summer eve
For all the love they both cultivated, she knew her days were numbered
He longed to bring her below but would never dream of dragging her
there; for it must be her choice, or he would never forgive his selfishness
The mortal wept, for she would not survive being apart from her love
Though felt fiercely worried about what horrors would greet her in hell
The Devil wiped tears from the soft eyes of his mortal, sullied with pain
The mortal nestled her face deep into his neck, silently breathing him in
The Devil held her, would hold her for a thousand years if she desired it
Swaying them both gently side to side, easing her weeping little by little

The mortal looked up at his rugged face and knew he would protect her
He would stay with her always, but she did not want him to bear that
burden
She knew it was a sacrifice for him to reside on Earth when he belonged
below
The Devil sensed her thoughts—as he so often did—and spoke against
her lips
It is no burden to do as my soul begs me, for I will never desire for you to
feel any pain; If staying brings you joy, I will forsake my duties and devote
all my days to you
She melted at his words and knew he spoke the truth, as he endlessly
would
As any lingering fears were washed away by the surety of their love
She let her Devil, her mate, her protector, lead her down to the under-
world
Knowing that with him by her side, she would never feel true fear again

Starlight Spirit

The lady of the river, a gaunt ghost, floats effortlessly upon the water
As if she is a part of the water herself, like one cannot exist without the
other
Outfitted only in flowing, stark white satin, her dress sparkles under the
moonlight
As if threads of starlight were sewn effortlessly into the fabric embellish-
ing her body
Though the pristine gown is in jarring contrast to her hollowed cheeks
and pale lips
And if she has any life left within her, she may shiver when the water
turns glacial
When the wind becomes wild, when nightfall settles in, deepening the
cosmic sky

Her frail hands, vacant of blood, trace the edge of a lone lily pad float-
ing beside her
And she ponders what the river is like during the day, a sight that she
will never see
Maybe the water ripples with delight, savoring the presence of wander-
ing creatures
Basking in the torrid heat of the sun, brimming with spirited life, burst-
ing with awe

The lady knows that she carries a deep sense of sorrow with her wherev-
er she goes
It is why she emerges from the trees only when the moon settles into
place each night
Becoming a starlight spirit, seen only by the river and the celestial sky
sparkling above
For she fears that when she appears, it is her presence that drives away
those creatures
Perhaps she sucks the life straight from the water like an unknowing,
innocent leech

Shame devastates her, horrified that she could be depriving the river of such liveliness
But the river quickly assures the lady she does not fault the spirit for the dejection she exudes
The river recognizes it within herself, and so she invites the ghost back, time after time again
They weep together, as sisters, free from prying eyes, alone with only the moon and her stars
Who are not fazed by their collective sadness, not as they live in such solitude in the sky

The lady of the river becomes overcome with emotion, crying deeply upon hearing this
Not knowing how she needed to hear the words of faultlessness until they were spoken to her
And though she felt at peace gliding through the river before, she now feels truly understood
Her sorrow will persist though the water and the stars, and the lily pads will always be there
Waiting for her to return every cosmic night, and that is a small pleasure amid her despair

Captain of the Sea

Undying pirate captain, destined to live an illustrious life, designed for daring thrills
Confidently sailing upon his charmed ship, spelled to never sink beneath the waves
Entirely eye-catching: a tall, imposing figure standing aboard the vessel
All rough edges, with calloused hands that raked through his wavy, windswept hair
Everything about him was tough and threatening, bursting with a sense of danger
Still his eyes may betray a faint glimmer of benevolence if one looks close enough
Listen to his voice, low and guttural, forever hoarse from shouting orders to his crew
His commands move through the air like a hurricane, impossible to ignore or to deny
Sunlight followed his every movement, attempting to trail after his magnetic stature
Some balk out of fear while others shy away due to a fawning desire they wish to hide

But one did not balk at all, for the woman—a stowaway—basked in his exploratory stare
Openly reveling in the way he repeatedly let his gaze run down the length of her body
Pining to explore the world, she only wished to travel as far as the sea would take her
Naturally she was discovered aboard only an evening ago, shaking from the arctic air
With one intense look into her eyes, the daunting captain granted her permission to stay
Now, stalking straight toward her, his jewelry chimed with each resolute step he took
Without a preamble, he declared that he believed he could love no one but the shining sea
A sea that never faltered, never failed him, continually moved with him, never against

Not even the priceless, invaluable treasure they were in pursuit of seemed as enticing
As the thought of swimming to the bottom of the sea and living out his immortality there
Asking if he still felt that to be true, the woman followed where his gaze had strayed
Expecting the pirate to be gazing out at the turquoise waters with blatant reverence
Though he only looked unsure, and she longed to steady his thoughts, ease his mind

Hastily he seized her wrist as she reached out a hand, his rings digging into her flesh
Dragging his eyes from the water to her lips to her eyes, she felt dizzy with attention
He was so close that if she dared to lean in further their mouths would gently meet
Though she did not have the chance to do so, for she suddenly gasped in realization
Knowing now that he looked at *her* with the admiration she thought belonged to the sea
Quietly urging him to answer, at last the pirate loosened his steady grip upon her wrist
Only to rub his palm over the spot he had grasped, leaning in until his lips met her skin
Grey eyes boring intently into hers, his wet, indecent mouth, rasped intimately into her ear
My stowaway, I believe the sea can never love me back in a way that I sus-pect you can; the water brings us safely to shore, but I think that you could bring me to my salvation
With those words, the pining pair knew that while the pirate still had an eternity to live
For the rest of her mortal life, his stowaway would stand beside him, sailing the world
Gazes never again straying to the sea, for they will only wish to look upon each other

Deadly Kiss

I knew the taste of your lips would be fatal; you told me time and time
again
But when you placed your mouth against mine, I could not imagine
resisting
As your reckless, deadly kiss invaded my body and brain, I accepted my
fate
Had I not known it would end this way? Had I not dreamt of this very
moment?

Your venom moved down my throat, lining my airways, threatening to
suffocate
My lungs heaved with the effort to keep breathing, gasping for more
and more air
The taste of copper began to flood my senses; warm blood soon filled
my mouth
Escaping faster than I could stop it or will it to go back into my body,
into my veins

My blood began trickling onto my collarbones, falling like rain in a
thunderstorm
Soon my skin became bathed in red, like a meadow crowded with scar-
let dahlias
My body was frozen—a block of ice; I felt as though I would never be
warm again
Overwhelmingly unstable, my eyes could barely stay open and my pulse
was faint

Long, torturous moments passed, and miraculously I began to breathe
once more
Though I feared the venom may not have been venom at all, but some-
thing far worse
For my skin stayed cold, my heart ceased its beating, and I acquired an
unending thirst
I worried that only one thing, red and gory, would satiate this uncon-
trollable craving

Looking up, shaken and dazed, I found you staring at me with pride
and exhilaration
At that moment your sharp fangs shot down, revealing themselves to
me without shame
And I knew that your kiss was deadly indeed, but it had not taken
everything from me
For I had emerged as something else, something insatiably sinister:
alive, and yet not
Mere moments of your fatal mouth pressed against my own, and every-
thing changed

Forgotten Gods

High in the sky, a world away, lived the great gods
Lazing in Olympus, their duties carelessly abandoned
Though they were meant to watch us from the clouds
Ordained to selflessly service in our times of desperation
The divine idols, fickle as ever, took to relaxing instead
Idly lounging, quietly conversing, peacefully sleeping
When they laughed until breathless, the Earth shook
When they cried somber tears, the oceans overflowed
They did not hear our screams, the echoes of our cries
Our voices were thick with anger, heavy with anguish
They did not perceive us, or they simply did not want to
Eventually the forgotten gods took to forgetting us too
Heavenly intervention was as rare as the gods themselves
Our plights appeared too mundane, our troubles too slight
War and famine persisted, and still, aid never came our way
As we stumbled through life, the gods swiftly turned away
When we drowned, gasping for air, they closed their eyes
Pray if you must, but speak only to the sky, the sun, the stars
For there is no one else above, no gods at all, who will listen

Angels Condemn, Demons Praise

Euphoria and damnation are drawn to each other
Much like a fluttering moth to a sweltering flame
A sinner feels more bliss in violence and vengeance
Than an angel feels in sanctifying and consecrating
The Devil does not fall prey to the horrors of his world
He sees the glory within the depraved, the uninhibited
Demons may not be pious or adorn weighty wings
But they will never hide themselves behind masks
Heaven waits for you to atone, hell only welcomes
Angels ceaselessly condemn, demons lustfully praise
There is no real pleasure to be found within heaven
Only an eternal life doomed to live behind silver gates
Though they look more like confining bars from within
The Devil wants neither your pity nor your sympathy
For the underworld is not the atrocity you think it to be
When the Devil offers salvation in the form of freedom
Hurriedly trail behind with no hesitation or repentance
Watch rampant embers of flames lead the way to hell
Feel them stoke the fire burning in your boiling blood
Igniting your body more than any angel ever could try
Be a sinner bathing indulgently in the sheen of hellfire
Take the rough hand of the Devil, follow him down
Decadently sin, and finally delight in genuine ecstasy

Power

The witch had power beyond belief, consuming every inch of her very
being
One scant touch and she could decimate the world, crushing whole
civilizations
One soundless incantation and the witch could bring men down to
their knees
Though she hoped she would never desire to use her power for anything
evil
All too certain of what she was capable of, people gazed upon her and
recoiled
Others saw the witch and sought to bind her, to use her power for their
own needs
In their eyes she was a tool rather than a person—an object rather than
a human
But women will attest that thoughts of that kind are not limited only to
witches
Harsh looks such as these were far too common to illicit a response
anymore

Until one day, beginning just like the rest, as clouds parted to reveal a
rising sun
The witch met a stranger who looked at her in a way no one else ever
dared to
Staring brazenly with no dread, no ulterior motives, just boldly consid-
ering her
As daunting as she normally appeared to be, the witch suddenly felt
paralyzed
Frozen, refusing to break the stare of this stranger, addicted to his atten-
tion
While others made her ashamed of her power, he simply helped her
accept it
With how intensely he gazed, longing to swim in the waters of her dark
eyes

He walked toward the witch ever so slowly, giving her a chance to
retreat
But bubbling with unexpected anticipation, she had no intention of
moving
She stayed rooted to her spot like a seed finding purchase in a patch of
soil
With courage, she spoke just loudly enough for him to hear, *do you fear
me?*
Before she finished asking, the witch already knew the answer within
her soul
He confirmed this by instantly responding, *do you fear the sun in the sky?
Hotter than a thousand flames, yet it delivers us nothing but a blissful
warmth*

Smiling, the witch did not bother asking any more questions; she did
not need to
He saw her for who she was, with charms and spells swirling around in
her mind
And she knew that he would never recoil from her power, never stifle
her magic
She knew he would love her—powers or not—and that thought eased
her own fears
Granting her relief that she would never shatter the world, not with him
by her side

Rose Fairy

In this peaceful garden, a veritable paradise amid an undisturbed meadow
Here lives a rose fairy, no bigger than a silver thimble, no smaller than a seedling
Flowing hair as red as her tiny, fierce heart, she effortlessly blends in with her roses
Watching over the lush patches of soil, warding off evil spirits and vengeful ghosts
With a snap she casts a spell, allowing her magic to merge as one with the garden
The enchantment travels below the sopping dirt, wraps around every root, each seed

Doubt plagues the fairy, as she is relentlessly terrified her magic will not be enough
And so she stays awake and aware, devoting her life solely to the enamoring flowers
Temperate and unassuming, though she would endure anything to keep her roses safe
Wholeheartedly she protects every petal of every flower as if she bore them herself
She would shed her own flesh and drain her own blood if ever the roses asked her to
When the wind grows violent, she drapes her wings over the delicate roses, as shelter
When the rain threatens to drown, she opens her mouth and drinks each droplet that falls
When the sun is hidden by a patch of clouds, she offers light to the blooming flowers

Summer comes and goes, but the fairy dutifully remains resting upon the autumnal dirt
Waiting for the leaves to change and the snow to fall so spring may once again return
Springtime air coaxes the flowers from the ground one by one by the magic of nature
As the fairy keenly watches, stems arise, strewn with prickly thorns that lead to a bud
Which then blossoms into a rose, composed of petite petals awash with a ruby hue

Although the garden is filled with plants of every kind, only the roses will grow tall
Blossoming fruitfully and demanding the rapt and devoted attention of all who visit
While the rose fairy looks on close by, boundlessly watching and guarding and loving
And the roses—so perfectly crafted—love her back just the same, perhaps even beyond
After all, they grow every season without fail, just to gaze upon their fairy once more

Eternity of Melancholy

Heartbroken, inconsolable vampire, forced to live eternally, fated never to be touched again
For anyone else's hands would feel like acid in comparison to his lover's heavenly touch
His beautiful mortal, delicate as a petal, sweet as pure honey, had left his side far too soon
Although perhaps no amount of time, not even forever, would have felt like long enough
Even when she was alive he had begun to miss her, grieving the loss he knew was inevitable
Year after year he lamented over his immortality, cursing himself to an eternity of melancholy
He longed to lie beside her beneath the dirt, to hold her cold hand in his until the end of time
His pain persisted, as it always would, though he tried to carry on, to keep her memory alive
The vampire grew weak, and he knew he must feed, but blood had lost its tantalizing appeal
For he did not want to sink his teeth into another and feel their pulse beat beneath his tongue
A reminder that there were so many among the living, while his lover was mournfully gone
Nights were tainted with misery; even the radiance of the moon did nothing to lift his spirits
Women saw his forlorn expression, his sullen eyes, and coyly longed to help, to cure his pain
He batted them all away, night after night, as if they were nothing more than pestering flies
Buzzing around his head, reminding him of the gaping hole within his aching, shattered heart
Already undead, the vampire felt as if this was a second death more horrific than the first
A raw, throbbing ache consumed him, and for the first time in centuries, he felt disoriented
No thirst for blood, no lustful desires, and no thoughts in his mind, save for his departed lover

All at once the vampire remembered a moment soon after they had first fallen into love

She had asked him, *Do you wish that I could live endlessly so we would never have to part?*

The vampire answered with distress in his heart, yet surprisingly, his voice did not waver

I would not wish the curse of immortality upon you, for my soul would surely break for you

If you had to endure the evils of this world, the agonizing injustices for centuries, millennia

But when you leave this realm, I will follow, and I will never part from you, even in death

For our souls are intertwined in an imperishable way, and for that I am immeasurably grateful

And so, heart full of woe, bones throbbing with grief, he sullenly walked toward his coffin

The vampire stepped inside, laid down his tired body, and shut himself in calming darkness

Vowing never to leave, not until his body left this cruel world and joined his lover in the next

And it was only that thought, that hopeful dream, that let the vampire drift into a restless sleep

An eternity passed, and his broken heart decayed into dust and his mind fell into a deep darkness

His life among the living, full of suffering and sorrow, had mercifully come to a permanent end

And it was his unshakable devotion that carried him straight into the arms of his beautiful mortal

Waiting for her vampire, still delicate as a petal, still sweet as pure honey, she embraced him

Moving her mouth to his ear, she softly whispered, *I knew you would find me again someday*

The vampire stroked her cheek with tears in his eyes, for he thought he may never do so again

As his heart healed, he knew with true certainty that his eternity of melancholy was over at last

Grim Reaper

In the dark of the night, the Grim Reaper dragged his scythe along the
bark of the trees
The jarring sound grating upon the ears of the hummingbirds escaping
to quieter lands
Death flowed within his veins like waves within a sea, fueling his heart,
guiding his feet
He did not savor bestowing this terrible fate upon the unsuspecting, yet
he knew he must
For as long as the world turned, he was shackled to this solemn, con-
stant responsibility
As he takes the last breath straight from a stranger's mouth, he inhales
as deeply as he can
Swallowing the final remnants of their life, feeling it settle in the pit of
his leaden stomach
And as death washes over them, consumes them, he closes his eyes,
moving on to the next

The valiant huntress vowed never to die, never to be captured by the
frigid snare of Death
Life violently pounded through her veins, willing her heart to never
cease in its beating
The huntress caught glimpses of the Grim Reaper over the years, yet she
was never afraid
In order to live—to survive—she could not let fear seep inside her
bones, lest it devour her
The huntress knew she would only find true peace once the reaper him-
self met his own end
She began to search for him, and when they crossed paths, that is when
the chase began

The Grim Reaper, doomed to a life of destruction and demise, rejoiced
at these hunts
He marveled at the tenacity the huntress exuded in running straight
toward death incarnate
He always evaded her, but only just barely, for he enjoyed the excite-
ment of the chase

Over time he marveled at more than just the unyielding determination she displayed
He dreamt of her auburn hair, blowing behind her as she ran with the gait of a gazelle
He longed to stop for just a moment to see if she might stride into his hopeful arms
To see if, in her lack of fear, she could love him—something he never wished for before
So as she chased him once more, the Grim Reaper slowed his pace, turned, and waited

The huntress did not hesitate, did not give herself any time to wonder why he had stopped
She merely aimed her bow and watched closely as her penetrating arrow pierced his heart
As she knelt beside his broken, bleeding body, she questioned the look of heartbreak he wore
I thought I found my match in you, the only one who ran near, never away, the reaper rasped

In that one moment, the huntress knew that he loved her, though she could not say the same
Instead she indulged her adversary in a moment of softness and wiped his fallen tears away
The fading Grim Reaper gave her a pained smile before joining the very souls he had taken
She trembled as his icy death washed over her, inside and out, though quickly she recovered
The huntress picked up his scythe, dragging it along the bark of the trees, finally at peace

Satanic Love Affair

He was the Devil, tempting me with fire; I was an angel, already igniting the flame
He was the embodiment of chaos and wrath, while I was supple and sweet as licorice
When he spoke wicked words against my gasping lips, I begged for total damnation
The Devil held a power over me that I could never truly understand nor did I want to
Panting with desire, he gripped my face, urging me to stare into his pitch-black eyes
Whispering, *do not pretend to be an angel when you belong with the demons in hell*
He was right, for my bone white, saintly wings did not seem to fit me any longer
I knew we would be happier in the shadowy underworld among the burning flames
Than we would be lazing upon a cloud in heaven among the doves and docile saints

Anger and bitterness grew within my shifting soul as my blood ran frenzied with rage
Incited by my Devil but directed at the world above for everything it took from me
Making no attempt to placate my loathing, he merely brushed my hair from my neck
Moving his mouth across the column of my throat, murmuring quiet encouragement
With steel in my eyes, I began to take from my world exactly as it had taken from me
It was then that my Devil knew I was ready to be carried from this realm into the next
Finally ready to travel to a world with brimstone in the air and coals lining the ground

Eager to bring me to his place of depravity where anarchy reigned, he
touched me
And my anger ebbed into craving, for though the face of the Devil was
malevolent
His carnal, invigorating touch was anything but, and I grew impatient
with wanting
Wanting his hands, wanting his mouth, wanting to journey to hell and
remain there
For once we descended, our affair would turn wanton in the most deli-
cious of ways

My Devil would place me atop his lap, upon a throne of skulls, among
all the sinners
We would let gluttonous bloodlust and intense passion pour over our
writhing bodies
Lips coated in blood, necks pierced open, fires erupting from the heat
of our devotion
We would be surrounded by cruel demons and feel fueled by the atroci-
ty of their sins
With each evil offense, our hunger for wickedness would grow in tan-
dem with our love

The Devil had not intended to corrupt my sweet soul, but from the first
lustful touch
From the first ravenous kiss we shared, we both knew we would never
be able to stop
We longed to go through life and death connected, body and soul, no
matter the cost
A mischievous, knowing look spread across the Devil's face as he took
my hand in his
Knowing a trip to hell would ensure rejection from heaven, and yet
both we felt no fear
As we tumbled down, filled with pure yearning, tangled together, eu-
phorically rebelling

Witches of Darkness

Mistress of the moon, lover of the stars, goddess of the night
Spellbound, watch as the magic in the air awakens and ignites
Open your eyes to the potent power of what lies within the dark
Seek out all that hides within the shadows and silhouettes of dusk
Let the dark enchantments confine you in their mystical bondage
Cast a spell to the unearthly protectors of nightfall dwelling above
Speak freely to the deities of twilight, the witches of darkness
Entrance and enrapture all those who are desperately drawn to you
Mesmerize them, lure them in with sugary words they thirst for
Bewitch, charm, mystify, let the incantations consume your soul
Until they are as vital as your beating heart beneath your flesh
Gasp at living art residing within the vast, darkening, cosmic sky
Marvel at stars shaped like jewels, crafted like delicate dewdrops
Look upon the full moon, exponentially glowing with every spell
Beaming fiercely with every love potion brewed and swallowed
The scent of magic is in the air, sweeter than the taste of sugar
The moon will hear; the stars will watch; the night will reply
You only have to close your eyes and incline your head up high
For the witches of darkness are always speaking directly to you
Whispering their words into your ears, hoping you will listen

Gods and Mortals

Deities from realms high above and down below
Glided down, sadistically ready to feel our woe

The god of mirth slyly masqueraded himself as the joker
Yet to give the gift of true delight, he could not yet broker
Moving past weeping mortals, a smile painted upon his face
Snickering, while his deceptive mask was firmly set in place
Such selfish delight moved steadily through his immortal veins
Glad to be a god, for mortals latch onto grief as if bound by chains

The queen of the gods transformed into an empress, stunningly regal and bold
Superiority shone through her eyes, compelling all mortals to submit to her hold
The empress looked upon her new subjects, mortal and frail and worse for wear
And hoped that all could feel her stifling sense of dominance strangling the air
As they curtsied, wailing mortals watched as their tears fell straight to the floor
For even in the presence of captivating power, their agony lingered evermore

The angel of love split in two and in an instant became the lovers
They moved through this world watching so very closely all others
Those fretting that the fiery love they feel would one day stop burning
Those sharing longing glances, only to never give in to their yearning
Mortals loved cautiously, surreptitiously, their desires never to be spoken
While the lovers sang aloud brazenly, alerting every ear to their devotion

All around them, Death dutifully lingered, not bothering with a clever
disguise
For mortals never sense him until they are gazing into his serpentine
eyes
He hunts this realm with a shrewd look casting a shadow over his grim
face
Knowing distressed mortals will soon walk right into his fatal embrace
As the entertained deities from faraway worlds start to float away
Death stays behind until he can free the mortals from the cold light of
day

When their time is up, the mortals will rejoice and cheer
For all that surrounded them in life was sorrow and fear
And as they turn into deities themselves, transforming
They will think to travel to our world, take to performing
Disguised, they will gape at the face of a mortal, so blue
And suddenly forget that they once had felt that way too

Tears of a Vampire

Vampires are doomed to live in the shadows, to become one with the
darkness
To never feel the warmth of the sun beating down upon their cold,
sallow skin
Shrouded in a life full of despair and desperation, beleaguered by im-
mortality
Eventually they mourn and grieve the enthralling prospect of falling in
love
For every lover they take will drown in the despair that follows the
undead
They wonder how long love can truly last between the undead and the
living

For vampires love lasts long enough to feel the sting of heartbreak for an
eternity
Mortals are fortunate to have such finite lives, as their pain will one day
end
While vampires dutifully carry each painful memory, every
heart-wrenching loss
Like permanent bricks on their backs, weighing on them until their feet
long to rest
No longer willing to walk alone, they plead for their immortality to
irreversibly fade
For the gift of death would be a kindness, one they would happily,
greedily accept
But such a miracle will never come to pass, for the creatures have no
soul to offer
And the harbinger of demise has no desire for a body free of inebriating
mortality

So when the moon emerges each night, the vampires will despondently awaken
And when they feel that initial pang of bloodlust, they will weep wretched tears
Their hearts seized beating long ago, but their eyes can still cry all the same
This is the miserable, unrelenting cycle that these bloodthirsty beings must endure
Irreversibly undead, dreadfully longing for a life they will never again get to live

Shadow

She was true darkness, a shadow brought to life
Existing only in the dead of night, in true twilight
Nothing more than a silent silhouette, a dim shade
Illuminated only by the glow of the waning moon
Gliding through life unnoticed, undetected by all
Made only of dusk, of the air that fills the night
She bore no blood inside her boneless skeleton
With neither flesh nor a heart, only dark, vacant eyes
The shadow moves soundlessly, always spying
Storing secrets as if they are shards of polished gold
Merging into walls with the ease of an apparition
Gliding down long corridors with an innate ease
All who hear whispers of her powers—her skills
Beg to utilize her for their own egotistical needs
But the dark shadow only desires to remain alone
Gliding through the world without a word spoken
While saving the words others so hastily revealed
She does not use these stolen secrets against them
For residing within a world of such genuine darkness
She merely longed to hear of what happens in the light

Vitriolic Viper

Vixen, viper with vexing eyes and a vacant soul
Unconstrained inhibitions, torturous temptation
Luring you in, coaxing you into total submission
Wrapping you stringently around her lithe fingers
Rigorously coiling with every moment passing by
Sensual voice cutting through mist atop the icy sea
Remaining just under the water, watching, waiting
All know that the embodiment of evil lurks below
Hidden away only by the stealthy shadows of night
Nevertheless, all feel her wickedly deviant presence
Even the gentle moon is grateful for the distance
For it, too, is wary of the sinister aura she exudes
Wraithlike, no more than a spectral spirit of the sea
Never spotted until it is too late, your fate is sealed
Vitriolic viper, poisoning you from one single touch
Even still, you dare to swallow the venom willingly
If only so you may remain in her vindictive clutches
For merely one blissfully euphoric moment longer
Her sharp bite feels better than a caress from all else
The feeling of her full lips upon your wrist lingers
Like a permanent engraving written upon your skin
Soon, her poison rapidly streams into your blood
And you look up into her cold, serpentine eyes
Longing to thank her for holding your wilting body
Forgetting too soon it was she who weakened you
The vixen watches you pityingly, though not kindly
As your pulse grows nonexistent, your organs failing
She lays your body down and silently swims away
Leaving no trace, as if she had never been here at all
And as your dying heart quietly beats one final time
The heart of the viper carries on as steadily as ever

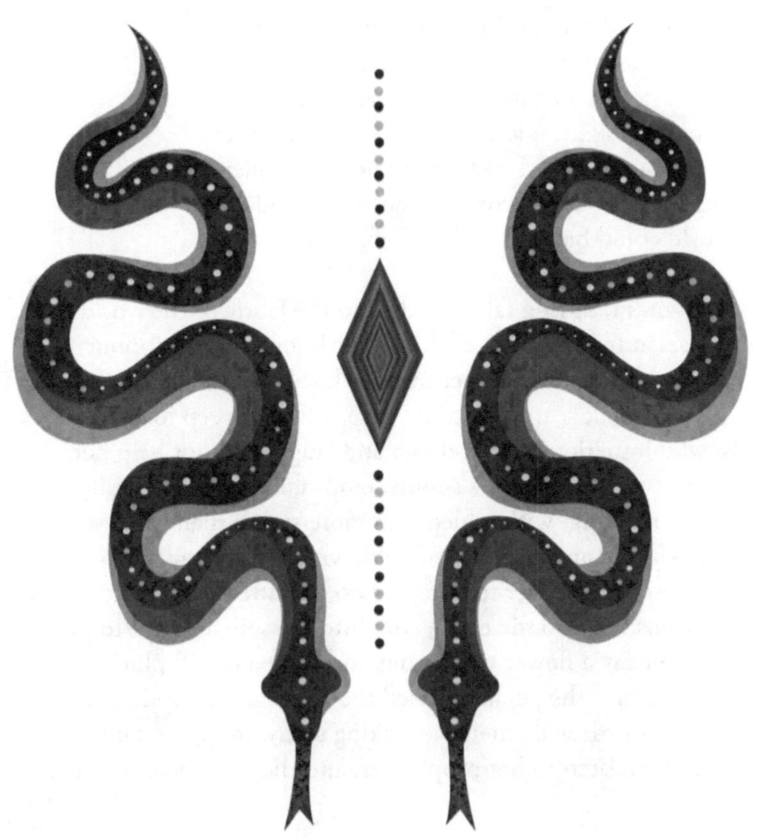

Cassandra

Poor, pretty Cassandra, all-seeing, none believing
Brain bleeding with every prophecy she learns of
Plagued with pain each time visions fill her mind
Thoughtfully place a tender truth upon her tongue
Mournfully watch it slip straight from her mouth
Listen as her warnings crumble to nothing but ash
With each word she speaks aloud, cautioning all
Imprisoned, a living ghost, you may touch her flesh
But her voice gets lost in the wind every day and night
For all her foresight, it amounts only to such misery
Never truly understood and never faithfully believed
Begging all to hear her words, to heed her guidance
The world could be at its end and none would listen

Silly Cassandra, sewing false words into the fabric of the world
Naïve Cassandra, speaking of things she knows nothing about
Stunning girl, it is too bad her mind is filled with such poison
Apollo, who took as quickly as he gave, will not weep for her
Gods, who imperiously look down and laugh, will not help her
Men die despite Cassandra's shouts; crops fail despite her wails
Daughter of a king, with gilded eyes more seeing than the rest
Princess with an angelic voice of gold, wrapped around truths
Urgent words fall off her tongue, yet no one attempts to catch them
Her cautions fall into the earth, sink into the soil, attempt to grow
Maybe someday a flower will sprout and someone will pluck it
As they lean into the petals to smell the sweet and tempting sap
Cassandra's words will emerge, speaking softly, though strongly
And they will listen to her prophecies, and they will believe her

Divine Dionysus

Dionysus: dizzy, drunk, and devious
Worship at the feet of Dionysus, climb the growing grapevines
Search for his rich, potent wine, swallow the psychedelic liquid
Pour it down your wanting throat; eat the juicy fruits of his orchards
Let their honeyed nectars drip down, making your skin so sticky sweet

Traipse throughout his open woods, feel the pleasure the forest holds
Watch the trees become animated the moment you speak his name
The words on your tongue will entrance even the smallest of sprites
Touch his cheek; feel his divine flesh and be met with salacious ecstasy
Rest your body down upon his altar, delight in the wild air of the night
Engage in his inebriated bacchanals, so dizzying you will soon see stars
Fervently bind your willing soul to his, commit to a life of intoxication

Collapse to the ground, lightheaded, wait for his hand to lift you up
But, too engaged in his many rituals, his strong hand will never appear
Still, you laugh into the soil, grateful to lay upon dirt he has walked on
That ceaseless, consuming devotion is the danger of his hallowed cult
It is a hazard all will be wrapped up in, but none will ever long to escape

Achilles and Patroclus

Haughty, arrogant Achilles; devoted, patient Patroclus
If only Achilles had luxuriated within Patroclus's love
Let it consume him, making him blind to everything else
If only he had a heart that beat solely for his truest lover
And quick feet that moved solely toward his other half
If only he did not have a heart that beat for recognition
And quick feet that walked swiftly toward his reputation
He would have never contemplated joining that war
For a life free of fame would have suited him just fine
As long as he was promised a long life with his lover

The way Achilles felt for Patroclus was never in doubt
He loved Patroclus with a soul-deep, crushing intensity
He adored him with every last bone in his warrior body
It was merely a matter of whether that love was enough
Enough to sustain his aching need for lasting notoriety
To be remembered, to be a fighter, to be a brave hero
Though what good are the songs they will sing for you
If your love is not there to sit beside you, listening too
Telling you that he loves you so, as he holds your hand
When Patroclus left Achilles—when he left this world
So too did Achilles leave, not his earthly body, not yet
But his soul followed Patroclus right into the next life
Holding on tightly, swearing never to leave his side
And for once, through true love, Achilles never did

Goddess of the Moon

Selene, goddess of the Moon and mother of vampires
White, voluminous hair adorned with a jeweled crown
Silver diamonds bejeweled within the lavish headpiece
Resting just above the eternal mark of a crescent moon
A mark that is brandished upon her brow, seen by all
Titan goddess riding high atop an enchanting chariot
Pulled through the sky by a cluster of feathered mares
Creator of intuition gifting insight in times of dire need
Deity who visits dreamers to offer wisdom and guidance
Selene admires the glossy and gleaming sky each night
From her rightful place, perched upon the ethereal moon
She softly shines her luminescent light down to Earth
Hoping to touch the souls and hearts of every vampire
Those who were born from her very blood, her very life
Look to the sky and feel Selene's aura descend upon you
And realize that you are never truly alone when dusk falls
For the goddess of the Moon and the mother of vampires
Will always be there to guide you in the depths of darkness

Undying Guilt

Everlasting is the plight of a vampire, not unlike that of their undying
lives
Sensing the potent scent of guilt in the air with every life they ruthlessly
take
Yet they will never stop; they never can, for their appetites will only be
satiated
With the consumption of warm, human blood, thick with mortal life
and energy
Though the creatures of the dark are often plagued by emotions of deep
dishonor
Their need for blood is far stronger, and they would go to any lengths to
indulge

If a vial of life—a small potion crafted solely to cure them of their end-
less affliction
Sat before them, so closely within reach that they could smell the mysti-
cal contents
The vampires would not let one drop fall upon their tongues saturated
with blood
They know that despite the shame and sorrow they will always carry
inside of them
The heady feeling of being inebriated off bloodlust is worth the regret
that follows
And this total disregard for morality and decency will continue to haunt
the undead
It will follow them every night, with every bite, century after century
after century

Coven

A coven so alluring, even the stars are trapped under their spell
Three seductresses, witchcraft bursting from their immortal veins
Lips dripping with magic, tongues heavy with unspoken charms
Intoxicating witches, feel high from their hallucinogenic touch
Magnetic eyes, entirely enamoring until all became infatuated
Lilting voices, whispering incantations beneath a blood moon
Follow them all to the ends of the world in deep, dark devotion

The first, with raven hair as black as a demon's soul, as smooth as silk
Falling down her back in loose waves, tinted with streaks of true red
Her powers invoke flames; her blood flows with a flickering fervor
Summoning heat as the air grows frigid and bleak once night falls
Infernos dutifully surround her, though they never burn her flesh
Fire answers to her very presence, fiercely hot, motivated to please

The second, with golden hair made of starlight, wispy like gossamer
Pulled back into an intricate updo, the envy of all those who pass by
Her magic calls to water; her heart beats to the rhythm of the sea
Commanding the rain, the rivers, the ravines, all to her own will
Oceans can be tamed only by the sound of her elusive, soft voice
They listen dutifully, the tides rising and falling each day, for her

The third, with lush green hair the beaming hue of jade stones
Curly locks surround her face, messy, strewn this way and that
Her charm orders the air to do her bidding each day and night
With a quiet clap of her nimble hands, the wind blows, howls
Making trees sway, encouraging flowers to dance until dawn
The air belongs to her, tied to her magic, as it always will be

Do not fear the coven of witches, for they speak without malice
Invite them in, heed their words, feel their magic drift to the sky
Watch closely as the shadows of the night surround the vixens
Distressingly desperate to be under their spell like everyone else
Listen as the wind, the water, and the flames are brought to life
Unable to resist the heady power of the witches, for none can

Dark Embrace

Sweet, blissful angel, gently guiding you into a peaceful sleep
Or wicked, devious demon, coaxing you into the arms of evil
Close your eyes and tell me, do you see a tunnel of beaming light
Or an abyss of bleak darkness—a void of desolate nothingness?
Does depravity call to you, and do you desire to answer its cry?
Will you fall easily into a soft and soothing bout of slumber
Or will you lean in closer to the shadows lingering in the dark?
Can you leave heaven to visit hell, if only for a little while
And if you can, would you ever return? Would you want to?
Does hell, with its sinful flames, entice you more than heaven?
When a demon knocks on your door, will you politely let him in?
Light a candle to better illuminate his face, to study his features
Will you ask him about what lies below out of fear or interest?
He will take your hand and tell you everything you want to know
The demon will sit with you until the night starts to slip away
And when it is time to leave, he will look at you so intensely
Almost pleadingly, silently asking, begging you to join him
Quietly you will say, *not yet, not until I close my weary eyes*
And am met only with darkness will I then dare to join you
Wait for me, please, just until my light gradually leaves me
For the second it does, I will walk directly into your arms
And one day, free from any illusions of sugary sweet angels
You will hear the song of depravity and drink in its melody
Finding your demon—the very same who came to your door
Waiting for you, with more patience and trust than any saint
With arms outstretched, famished for the feel of your embrace
Only now, bathed in true darkness, will you go to him at last

Fortune Teller

The fortune teller, blessed with blood that carried potent magic
Yet cursed with the inability to cast even the slightest of spells
Resigned herself to a quiet life of crystal balls and tarot cards
The celestial atmosphere, laden with stars, guided her hand
Allowing her powers to come alive, not through any charms
But through the cards that sat before her: an otherworldly deck
Infused with her magic, the cards were gifted true knowledge

The Moon, galactic and grand, told stories of new beginnings
The Devil, always roguish, spoke of giving into temptation
The Fool, a nonsensical jester, mused of a cathartic journey
The Sun, sizzling hot, whispered of a joyous awakening
The fortune teller leisurely looked into her crystalline ball
And upon her touch it came to life, swirling with allure
At times it showed her visions of romantic tales of love
Brimming with barrels of sweet admiration and promises
Other times it showed nothing but grim tragedy and ruin
Teeming with the chilling essence of foreboding demise

For good or for bad, she poured her powers into her craft
And felt her magic grow with each deck she skillfully shuffled
Her truths were genuine; her warnings were sincerely authentic
If she could not recite the invocations she had so longed to
At least the clandestine sorceress could share her powers
Letting others drink from her cup of mystical knowledge
Warning them not to swallow too much, lest they choke
For seeing one's future may devastate just as it may mend

Blood on my Mind, Death in my Soul

Bloodlust enraptures me from the very first drop that settles upon my waiting tongue
The foreign taste is reminiscent of the most ambrosial of nectars and the finest of wines
I warily lift a finger to my bruised, reddened lips, swollen from sucking and savoring
And feel a prick upon my skin, proof of who, or what, I now am, what you have made me
With blood on my mind and death in my soul, I ponder if our love is worth this cost
Should others lose their lives so carelessly and sinfully, so we may live ours, together?
Immortality means nothing if guilt envelops me with every slashing bite that I take
Their blood should not belong to me and yet I need it, I crave it, more than anything
I want it more with each passing moment, for my mind is trapped within a gory haze
Though shame perpetually follows me, I will endure this fate, only for the one I love
Only for him will I drink, knowing his conscience is just as tainted with grief as mine
We will walk this world together, reassured that though the price was terribly grave
Our love will now never die, and that is one small mercy amidst all the bloodshed

Purgatory

Melancholy, miserable, morose ghosts
Will forever continue to wallow the most
Spirits effortlessly slip through thick walls
Moaning loudly of their innumerable pitfalls
Weeping, for the ghosts have nothing left to give
Wailing, mourning a vibrant life they can no longer live
Never again able to fall in love, never again to dream
Urgently wanting to speak, yet they can only scream
Miserably longing to touch and morosely pining to chatter
Begging to truly be seen, to tell someone what is the matter
They will reach out a pale hand only to find purchase with air
There is not much more that these despondent ghosts can bear
Trapped within a dizzying realm of in-between, not entirely life
And not entirely death, though the wind still howls there with strife
Wedged within an unresponsive world that they never did choose
The spirits will turn to haunting, and for this they have no excuse
Though they will never harm, they need something to focus on
Anything but their dreadful fate, or their mortal life, now gone
The ghosts are sincerely sorry for the tears they may trigger
They would much rather embrace you with voracious vigor
Pass by the ghosts and gift them with a fable or an allegory
Sit with them in the dark, free them from this purgatory
You cannot see, but they will rejoice at your attention
For your gentle words will ease their spectral tension
Their melancholy and misery may always remain
But now lessened is the heaviness of their pain

Gaia and the Devil

Gaia, goddess of Earth, fell in love with the Devil, ruler of the Under-
world
She loved his cunning mind, his razor-sharp wit, how he held her in the
dark
He loved her tenderness, the way she cared for every flower, every grain
of dirt
How she looked at him with such earnest commitment in her light,
gentle gaze
They loved as if they were both starved, as though they had been
parched for eons
Then wondrously found ravines of endless rivers in each other's eyes,
lips, touch
Only when they were wrapped up in each other did they feel their
burdens lessen
The obligations of their titles faded from their minds until they could
exhale at last
And when they did so, the deeply obsessed couple thieved each other's
breaths
Wishing to inhale the troubles constantly plaguing both of their lethar-
gic souls
Raring to carry their problems so both would feel only deep love and
quiet peace
And when Gaia reluctantly returned to Earth, weeping all the way to
her world
And when the Devil grimly returned to the Underworld, sullen with
stark longing
She touched a hand to her heart, conveying her adoration, and he
echoed the motion
Though they were separated by distant realms, when the wind passed by
just right
She swore she felt a whisper of his lips pressed against the aching nape
of her neck
And he knew he felt the faint touch of her soft hand holding securely
onto his own
Though they were worlds apart, their souls would cling to each other
through eternity

Chameleon

Chameleon, for her blood was everchanging, always transforming
One moment she was crystalline blue—a pristine, glistening pond
While the next she was olive green, mimicking thick summer grass
She had transformed into every color, every texture, every element
Known what it was to be bark upon a tree, wildflowers upon a hill
Though she had been seen by all, she felt entirely known by none

Once, as she was posing as sunlight—shimmering and sparkling
A man emerged, seemingly admiring the light before speaking
Your beauty is unparalleled, though I yearn to see your true form
He sighed softly, afraid of scaring her away, then patiently waited
She was stunned into silence, for never before had this transpired
Never before had anyone else seen through her convincing illusions
Only to display an authentic interest in *her*—in her genuine nature
She gingerly eased herself out of the snug facade of glaring sunshine
Shyly stepping into her natural body, so rarely used, so rarely seen
The man blinked, his eyes widening slightly, his mouth falling open
Instantly he reached out a shaking, hypnotized hand to touch her
Though he hastily stopped himself short, snapping out of his stupor
For he would not dare impose his sudden desires onto her uninvited
Astonished by his thoughtfulness, she reached out her own hand
Placing his right over hers, guiding him to her now blushing face
For a moment, they studied one another: wide eyes, tempting lips
She could not believe someone was looking upon her truest form
And yet he did not recoil from the chameleon, not in the slightest
He could not believe that he was so fortunate as to be here with her
That she was granting him this cherished, candid gift of vulnerability

The world seemed to stop then, so they could rejoice in this moment
Only when the birds sang again and the oceans resumed their waves
Did the man say with total sincerity, *please, do not disguise yourself*
For I will never wish to see you as anything other than exactly as you are
With rare tears flowing from her eyes, she leaned into his warmth
Nestling her head into his neck, feeling no urge to transform, to hide
Truthfully seen, fully known, they peacefully walked away together
As the true sun on the horizon began to shine brighter, just for them

Hunger

As the vampire drifted closer to my neck
I saw such hunger in their steel black eyes
And wondered about their gluttonous gaze
Did it speak of an urge to indulge in bloodlust
Or was it a yearning, almost nostalgic look
Desperate to satiate their mindless jealousy
Toward my wildly pounding human heart
Full of life, brimming with verve and vigor
Wishing that their cold, unmoving heart
Could beat one more time beneath their chest
And as they got closer to my thumping pulse
Trapped within my mortal body, my warm skin
Perhaps the vampire hoped that this closeness
This intimate touch, their mouth on my flesh
Might gratify that need to be alive once more
If only for a singular, breathtaking moment
But then they ravenously licked their lips
Tightening their lethal grasp on my throat
And I knew it was only blood they craved
Anything else, any remaining desire or plea
To be granted the fragile gift of mortality
Had drowned long ago, fatally sinking
Into an icy puddle of their victim's blood

Two Ghosts

The ghost dimly drifted from room to room, trapped in a wretched
cycle of doom
A forlorn life led to a harrowing end, and that despair followed the
spirit into death
The house felt hauntingly hollow, and so the ghost longed for a loyal
companion
Though he had none in life, and did not dare to believe that one would
find him now
Winter turned to spring, and weeping followed, yet it was not his own
that he heard

A new ghost appeared, frightened, confused, and deeply grieving the life
she had lost
Her quivering face was plagued with tears, born from a ceaseless on-
slaught of anguish
The old ghost tried hard to not show his bubbling elation, though he
was truly grateful
For this chance at friendship, and he lightly treaded so as to not startle
the new spirit

The ghosts began to share stories, divulging old hopes and dreams that
now seemed futile
Sometimes, through what must have been a miracle and nothing else,
they even smiled
Soon their tears dried long before new ones had the chance to appear
and stain their faces
These new tears were born only of joy and affection, all due to their
new, unending bond
Life was stolen from the pair too soon, but death gave them something
they never had: hope
The two ghosts now dreamily drifted from room to room, caught in a
perpetual vortex of love

Eyes of Stone

Medusa, naturally villainized, never treasured
Painfully punished, transformed into another
Her hair—her long, lustrous hair—was stolen
Replaced by serpents just as incensed as her
She was violated in the most barbaric of ways
Only to be left alone, to scream into the ether
To lament over what she so violently survived

Soon after, Medusa was punished, heartlessly
Yet her transformation was not the worst of it
It was that she was so wrongfully admonished
Forced to pay for the demonic sins of another
It is no wonder that Medusa acted as she did
Using her punishment to gain back control
To take back the total power and autonomy
That had once been brutally taken from her

All she longed for was to be rid of her sorrow
And it was retribution that brought her relief
Enacting vengeance helped her to move on
Instead of remaining stuck in the quicksand
Of her haunting memories, always looping
She never forgot, though revenge helped
As she stopped men dead in their tracks
With a merely one bitter and stony stare

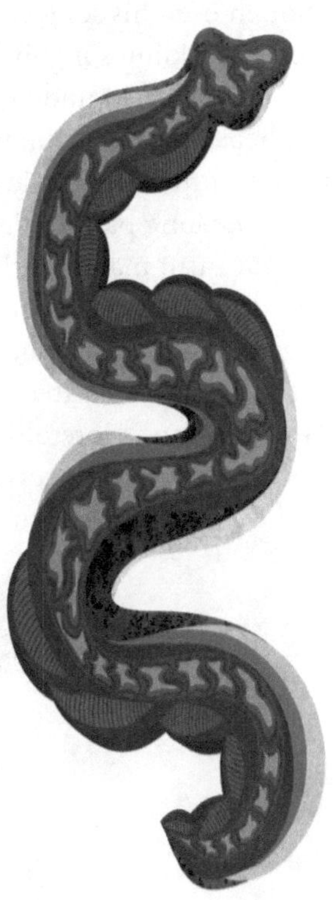

Medusa has just begun to feel a sense of peace
Only to then be killed, butchered, in the dark
As she was silently and serenely slumbering
Men rejoiced, thrilled from news of her demise
But women, they wept, awful, heaving sobs
For they ultimately knew that soon enough
This would indeed be their horrific fate too

Do Not Turn

Orpheus, love on his mind, a song in his heart, hope filling his veins
Eurydice, fire in her blood, hunger in her soul, lively as a hurricane
The Fates sang from the start that their love was bound for calamity
The deities prophesied long ago they would endure terrible tragedy
Him, gripping onto the lyre he cherished so, a fool with blind faith
Though even his song could not save her from becoming a wraith
Her, a sparkling songbird, taken away from this life far too soon
Her body carried underground, though she could still hear his tune
Orpheus, hopelessly infatuated, followed her down, ready to appeal
Hades, surprisingly in love himself, offered the pair a gracious deal
Walk the long path to life above, the fool in front, the bird behind
Do not turn; march until the sun leads you back to your own kind
Eurydice was not prepared for the pain that turned her vision black
When, of course, Orpheus, in a moment of hesitation, looked back
His face fell, devastated, her heart broke, crushed; they both wept
Although it was foretold, this was a fate neither could ever accept
His doubts would incessantly linger, which he would never admit
And their love, as resolute as it was, burned to ashes because of it

Burning Wings

Such an eager boy was Icarus, ever so filled with hope
Bursting with excitement, passionate for exploration
Blind to threats of danger, longing only to fly further

He climbed higher—too high—ignoring the dire pain he felt
The scalding sting of the sun, the wind whipping, slashing
His body was utterly ablaze, yet Icarus did not much care
For he felt as though the ether had rendered him weightless
His eyes held many tears from the sheer joy of truly flying
So content that the aches he felt did not faze him remotely

Icarus, they fretfully shouted, *come back*, they woefully wept
But Icarus only looked on as his false feathers came undone
Watching as they all soon fell, gently tumbling to the ground
A pleasant, pleasing sight, lined with such a terrible warning
His fate was regretfully sealed, just as the gods had declared
And he intended to fully live before his final, fatal descent

He closed his beaming eyes, hopeful right until the very end
And focused only on the sky—on the clouds touching his skin
The mist on his grinning face, the wind breezing by his body
And for one long, last moment, Icarus flew among the birds
And soared

Queen of the Underworld

Persephone, Persephone, Persephone
Those words sounded like a chant in the mind of Hades
The Fates report that the wicked king dragged Persephone
Down, down, down, to the chilling Underworld below
But she did not travel weeping all the while, not once
For the goddess of spring badly longed for a reprieve
From the glare of sunlight that unrelentingly followed
Taunting her about what she would never truly feel within
Hades, all dark and cold, did not desire to change her
To make her feel bright and warm, for he knew her well
The dark king, above all others, understood her darkness
He knew that a life full of depravity was what she needed

Hades stopped at nothing to bring her to the Underworld
Wanting to make her queen, needing to kneel before her
Bruising his knees praying to his beautiful, dark empress
Only in this realm, in the fiery halls, did her soul bloom
Blossoming in a way that the flowers above never could
She now pitied the sun and its light, the soil and its roots
For they would never feel the joyful relief of truly living
Of truly loving within the cover of endless, potent night
Hades lifted the pomegranate seeds to his queen's mouth
And Persephone, enveloped in such sinful shamelessness
Moaned as the tart juices from the fruit burst in her mouth
As she willingly swallowed them down, one by one by one

River of Reflection

Was it so wrong that Narcissus found solace and joy from within?
That one day, he looked upon his reflection in the moving waters
And burst into tears, weeping from the rippling splendor he saw?
Should everyone not be so kind to themselves as Narcissus was?
Should we all not live in shocking awe of our own, earthly beauty?
If vanity is a sin, then perhaps Narcissus was the very first sinner
He reveled proudly in the glistening hue of his bright, amber eyes
While you wallow in the dull, almost lifeless shade of your own
He spent his days basking in the radiance of his unblemished skin
While you spend yours weeping over the imperfections you see
Day after day, night after night, Narcissus adamantly remained
Staring into the cobalt water, admiring his immaculate features
And though he was mocked—none understanding his reverence
He did not once weaken; he did not falter or break his own stare
Narcissus stayed, gazing even in the smothering heat of summer
Even as snow fell upon his shoulders, as frost settled over his flesh
Only when he tumbled into the water, did his eyes briefly close
And during that moment of what should have been vast darkness
Narcissus saw his own image shining behind his lids, etched there
He smiled even as his lungs filled with water, as his heart slowed
The god of vanity died as he lived, drowning in perpetual bliss

Celestial Lovers

The god truly loved the goddess with an overwhelming intensity
He cherished her brilliant mind and kind soul with a deep devotion
She loved him just the same, as she had since the day they first met
The goddess awoke with his memorable voice echoing in her mind
And softly tumbled into sleep only if his body laid close beside hers
The other gods envied their love, eyes green with undiluted jealousy
Lost within their blinding romance, the pair left their defenses down
The other gods swiftly struck, and everything changed in an instant
The god was now a golden, blistering ball of light known as the Sun
The goddess was now a cosmic, glowing satellite known as the Moon

The Sun and the Moon wept, tears heavy with the pain of betrayal
Cursed with this solitary fate, they continued to yearn for each other
Their morose dreams consisted of nothing but thoughts of their love
When the Moon emerged each night, a silver and celestial beauty
The Sun sighed deeply with emotion, glad to catch a glimpse of her
Though he also tensed with torture, for they will never again touch
When the Sun emerged every morning, a luminous and gilded star
The Moon felt her bursting heart constrict with love and longing

The Sun began to grow tired of beaming down upon the Earth
He yearned to shed his boiling skin of the unrelenting gold light
Be free of the raging temperature thrumming beneath his surface
The Sun begged to feel a cool breeze dance over his fevered body
The Moon, sensing this, blew a strong wind through the night sky
Instantly chilling the Sun, gifting him a brief break from his heat

The Moon longed to appear as alluring as the stars around her
Though the silver luster she wore never quite felt like enough
Soon the Sun craned his neck to catch a glimpse of his love
Having sensed something was amiss, and acted without pause
The Sun took his own light and selflessly gifted it to the Moon
Refusing to stop until every star was wide-eyed, struck by awe
From the overwhelming glow that now surrounded the Moon

The lovers were so in tune with each other, loyally listening
Devotedly watching and encouraging, even from a distance
Though they could never return to being god and goddess
The pair were still hopelessly in love as the Sun and Moon

Look toward the hazy horizon just as day turns into night
And watch closely as the Sun lingers for a moment longer
Just to catch the fleeting sight of his only love, his Moon

Death

Death, unhurried and unbothered, searched for a man corrupted by gluttony
Ravenous for total control and absolute power, he was easy enough to find
For the putrid scent of gluttony and greed wafted from his body in abundance
Death grabbed the startled man by his neck without taking any care to be subtle
And plucked from him his life; it was as simple as picking a ripe cherry from a tree
The man, once full of authority and arrogance, now began to violently tremble
Regret began to settle into his cold bones as he realized his many mistakes
Death looked toward his latest victim, rolling his soulless eyes in indifference

What did you think would become of you? Did you think you would suffer no consequences?
Did you assume your mortal body was made to consume corruption at such a reckless pace?
Did you think your greed—your insatiability—would not eventually flood your fragile soul?
That it would not begin to seep from your pores, flow from your eyes, pour from your mouth?
That it would not leap at the inviting opportunity to devour you, to slaughter you, day by day?
Death scoffed as he finished speaking, amused by the predictable foolishness of all humans
The deceased began to plead somberly, *why did I wish for more? Why was I not satisfied?*
I continued to take and take and take, but now, it seems like I had more than I ever needed

A tense silence settled between the two men—well, between Death and his newly turned ghost

The ghost petulantly waited, hoping for a sense of closure before he descended into the afterlife

After a weighted, lengthy pause, Death answered with a deep and quite frankly frustrated sigh

You have an eternity to think of your many errors, I only hope you hunger no longer for power

The angels are not as merciful as you believe, for they will punish far worse than I ever could

The ghost, more panicked now than ever before, tried to cling forcefully onto Death's long cloak

Finding more relief in his presence than the idea of being alone, a spirit with no one to hold on to

Puffing out an irritated breath, Death pushed the ghost aside, deserting him in the shadows

As Death glided away, he felt glad—not for the first time—that he needed go no further

Witching Hour

The cosmic witching hour commenced
And straightaway I began to awaken
In the darkest moments of the night
Magic urgently beckoned me closer
Ancient power called to my blood
I was encircled by age-old spirits
Of all witches who came before me
Incantations coated my parted mouth
Begging to soon be spoken aloud
The divine power of enchantments
Lightly brushed against my shoulder
Like a reassuring and familiar hand
Guiding me toward what I needed
Transcendent is the sudden feeling
That overwhelmed me—dominated me
As magic found its way into my soul
And then I cried and cried and cried
The paranormal power cleared my mind
As it winded its way through my body
Infused itself into my bones, my veins
I knew now that I was my truest self
So spellbinding and utterly entrancing
Mercifully freed from my mortal chains
As the witching hour drew to a close
I brought forth the powers within me
And cast a spell, small and yet special
The words slipped straight past my lips
Landing upon the misty twilight air
Seeping into the earth—into the ether
Proudly wailing to all that is living
And quietly whispering to all that is not
On this night, as authentic darkness fell
My blood now buzzed as it never had
For I was born anew, a mystical witch

Coffin of Roses

Submissively slinking back into the shadows
once nightfall reaches daybreak
The vampire slips into his coffin as the first rays
of sunlight filter back into the sky
Rabid during the dark of the night, feverishly
hunting for fresh blood to consume
Though, when dawn emerges, he finds comfort
and peace inside his coffin of roses
Flowers the hue of blood adorn the onyx-painted
casket, charmed never to decay
Intricate carvings and macabre paintings cover
the coffin, all in shades of brilliant gold
Cobwebs cover the long surface in a layer of
fragile yet unsettling gossamer gauze
The vampire lifts the heavy cover just before the
sun rises, willingly climbing inside
Within, luxurious pillows line the lavish interior,
offering the contentment of a cloud
Though he has no need to slumber—not any-
more—the vampire will often doze off
For the calming feel of his coffin can carry even
the most undead of beings into sleep
Covertly hidden away, the ageless casket is kept
far from prying eyes and curious hands
Immersed in a mist of disorienting fog, it con-
tinues to remain a secret to mortal eyes
What a shame: that this creature will be the only
one to bask in the glory of the coffin
And glorious it will always continue to be, for as
long as the vampire lives, and beyond

Inconsolable Island

Inconsolable Island was occupied by none, haunted by all
Long ago the island was cursed to harbor terrible woe
Gloom skulked in, saturating the air upon the deserted land
Agony seeped into the dirt; flowers stopped blooming
The sun hid behind clouds; the rain was never-ending
Fruit grew rotten on vines just as quickly as it sprouted
Warmth evaded the island, replaced by a ceaseless chill
Day and night merged until the sky was perpetually grey
Ghosts grievously lurked about—even they longed to escape
So too did the rising tide, eluding high tide and the inland
For the water was all too ready to return to the sea

Time passed—years, lifetimes—and the gloom persevered
Having now sunk so far below the sand, beneath the soil
Until the ground, heavy with distress, gave way, cracking
Before suddenly sinking into itself, quickly and fervently
The island could not bear to stay upright any longer
And when the ground collapsed, finally fallen inward
Swallowed up by the pit of despair it had long cultivated
The island impulsively allowed itself to let out a small sob
Tears not born of sadness, but of an overwhelming relief
Freed from the ghastly curse, now bursting with true bliss

Enchantress of Stardust

She bursts with the romantic, reflective magic that fills the night sky
Gracefully soaring above the moon, her thighs skimming the cold surface
Breathing in all of the fantasies derived from the dreamers down below
Their reveries drift through the cosmos, past each cloud, across every star
Floating into the open mouth of the enchantress, ever so eager to consume
Beauty is synonymous with her name, a name even the sky never knew
Her body was crafted from magic—the very same that created the universe
Gleaming, an awe-inspiring aura obediently follows the witch through life
She exudes a complete and total power of the most ethereal and envious kind
The enchantress is light and dark; she is nothing and everything all at once
Shining, the witch is capable of shaping stars, meticulously molding them
On a whim she can magnify the luminosity of the moon to her own liking
Though above all else, she devotes her days to crafting iridescent stardust
That makes the vast stars glisten like no other within the immense cosmos
Grateful she can use the power she harnesses for something so very mystical

When the stardust is perfect, as if concocted by the cosmic gods themselves
Only then will she carefully immerse every star into the incandescent powder
With a steady focus that only a witch can possess, she coats each one in gold
Before placing the stars back into the sky with attentive and thoughtful care
And begin waiting for night to fall so all can marvel at her fragile creation
Though when she can, the enchantress of stardust silently marvels as well
Glowing with satisfaction, she is now ready to begin her work, once again

The Vampire and the Slayer

A vampire and a slayer fell in love, as if they had been crafted only to cherish each other
They fought their connection, yet the universe would not relent in bringing the pair together
The first time they met, during a moonlit night, more scenic than any night that came before
An unfamiliar heat moved through them, wholly unrelated to the sweltering summer air
Unsettled, they retreated to the opposite ends of the world, reluctant to give in to the spark
Yet thoughts of their meeting did not leave their minds or hearts, year after year after year
The slayer was meant to destroy her foe, erase his kind, and save the world from bloodshed
The vampire longed to sink his teeth into her supple skin, for her blood would taste heavenly
Soon they could no longer resist and began to secretly meet within the shadows of darkness
Though they were undoubtedly in love, their worries still haunted them like a chorus of ghosts
He still craved her blood, yet the idea of painfully piercing her skin made him sick with agony
She still felt an innate responsibility to protect and defend the innocent people of the world
Those considered inconsequential to the menagerie of monsters who would soon feast upon them
Still they could not stomach parting, for love conquered the couple as quick as a fevered plague
They now knew each other so intimately that while the vampire could not see his own reflection
The slayer saw him clearly enough for both of them, for his soul was mirrored within her own
She understood that their love tormented his lifeless heart, haunted with the fear of hurting her
For despite his adoring reverence, she was still human, filled with blood he would always desire

In an effort to ease his concerned worries, to prove that their love was stronger than his bloodlust
The slayer gently bared her neck to her vampire, inviting him closer to drink deeply and freely
Willing to give her love what he continued to crave if it meant that his mind would be at ease
She knew so confidently that he would not hurt her, would not drink a drop more than he needed
After all, the vampire would do the same for her if it meant they could live together in solitude
So the slayer brushed her glossy hair back, and the vampire bit slowly into her exposed neck
She watched in a trance as her blood painted his lips, then trickled down onto her pristine skin
When he dragged his mouth away, he grew frantic, worried her face would be twisted in pain
And only when he found nothing but love in her eyes did he finally sigh in deep contentment

To her surprise the slayer now felt empty from the frigid absence of his mouth on her neck
She would let him drain all of her blood if his lips could stay on her skin longer, forever even
Yet he would never take too much, for he loved her far more than he loved the way she tasted
As if sensing her thoughts, the vampire pressed a kiss of crimson against her jaw, whispering
I will crave you in this life and the next, even if your blood never sits upon my tongue again
For I would rather die of starvation than spend a single day with you not tucked into my side
The vampire, with dripping wet, cherry lips, and the slayer, with a neck marred with bite marks
Gazed at each other in a way that made the angels weep, vowing never to resist each other again

Darkness

A medley of candles sputtered to life within the abandoned room
The soft light teasing the darkness with the promise of company
The bleak emptiness in the space had turned into something living
Entirely tangible, desperate to escape the hopelessness in the room
The darkness forced its earthly, yet weakening body toward the door
Clawing, crawling toward the light, nails scraping across the floor
The exit was now slightly noticeable, revealing itself like a mirage

The darkness moved fiercely, gliding deliberately with such intent
That the movement created a faint though immediate gust of wind
A gust of wind that quickly moved straight toward the source of light
And wasted no time at all in extinguishing the already dying flames

The whisper of hope that had filled the room was thus destroyed
It quickly vanished along with the last wick within the last candle
The darkness once again became a weightless cloud of sheer shadows
Its soul too tired and its body too broken to remain whole any longer
In the abandoned room, it was fated to a life of sorrowful solitude
Never to be touched, never to be free, never to be corporeal again

Siren Song

The hypnotizing siren brazenly lies upon the rocky shore of the deserted beach
Her long cerulean hair settles in deep waves all along her slender neck and back
The warm tide reaches her legs, and she luxuriates in the water caressing her skin
Singing her captivating song, her voice rings out through the early morning haze
Hauntingly eerie, inherently exquisite; it is a melody that will never fade nor fail
Her otherworldly voice begins to weave into the mind of one unsuspecting man
Who now feels a profound pining as his feet move him in the direction of the song
The further he walks the more distant her voice becomes, just out of his eager reach
He runs, willing to walk atop flaming coals if it would bring him closer to *his* siren
For the man had begun to spin a tale that she was undoubtedly his, as he was hers
Believing the siren had willed her seductive voice to float through the air to find him
Certain her hands would soon roam over his skin, for that is what they were made for
Blinded by an infatuated obsession, he does not once falter as he continues his journey

After crawling inch by inch across the scorching sand, he reaches the queen of the sea
I heard your voice as if it was calling to me and me alone, the man drawls in a trance
In awe, his voice becomes quiet as he takes in her extraordinarily compelling beauty
Whoever hears my call is sure to follow, as it was decided by the fates, the siren sighs

From the corner of her eye, she notices the ire and chill that had crept into the water
What happens when they answer your call? the man whispers, eyes glossy, catatonic
Moving closer and closer to the waters of the turbulent sea, yearning to reach his siren
If they answer my call, it is already too late, she replies, sadness creeping into her voice
The man is dragged down below—yet another soul violently stolen by the raging sea
For the water only longs to have the seductress's attention for itself, never to be shared

The siren's mesmerizing gaze returns to the sea and the waves soon begin to calm
The water warms, and the jealousy within the water starts to wither away, for now
Though the siren revels in the sublime power of her beauty and her irresistible voice
At times she wishes that when the sea traps those who lovingly look upon the siren
As it carries them under, cruelly imprisoning, she wishes that the sea would take her too
Beneath the water that loves her so fiercely, perhaps the siren could finally finish her song

The Devil

Before his fall from grace, the Devil was once an angel, holy and blessed
But not even the most devout were immune to bouts of defiance, rebellion
The harsh price he paid in consequence was neither saintly nor pious nor just
His soft, cherished wings were slashed from his body violently, carelessly
He wondered, *what good is being an angel if you can be disgraced so viciously?*
Banished to hell—to a place of sin—where evil reigns supreme, his exile commenced

Now he sleeps on a bed of embers but does not speak of the pain when daylight comes
He welcomes the severe heat, the burn reminding him of everything he has endured
When night falls and wraps the Devil up in misery, only then will he start to weep
He cries for all he has lost, all that was taken from him, all he will never return to
He who sees more sin than any other and is expected to bear the burden of it all
Always isolated, never embraced, craving the reassuring touch of another's hands
Yearning for gentle words to be whispered to him when the agony becomes stifling
All alone, rupturing from the tremendous demands placed atop his weary shoulders

It is only the biting thoughts of revenge that keep the Devil standing
tall in hell
With calculated vengeance on his mind and agony pulsating through
his tired bones
He leads hell with the ferocity of someone who was wrongly punished
so long ago
Someone willing to inflict pain if it means being free from a fraction of
his own hurt
Hell becomes more and more wicked, century by century, as the Devil
bides his time
Waiting, longing with anticipation, for the day he can vindictively
storm into heaven
Letting the hallowed angels witness the monster they have molded him
into

Incantations

Your spell will not work if the intent is not clear
Crafted with a conflicted mind, torn in every way
The incantation can be spoken with perfect diction
Yet if your soul is tainted with irresolute indecision
Then only the cruelest chaos will be born soon after
Witchcraft is fickle; it requires a firm, strict resolve
Cast a charm with your wavering heart in disarray
And watch closely as the world worsens in return

Deserts tirelessly yearn for a single drop of water
For rain no longer deigns to descend from the clouds
Raging fires scorch and singe your incendiary flesh
As the flames swiftly incinerate each and every land
Fruitful crops turn rancid, nauseated with such decay
Aching with a raw, ravenous hunger and greedy thirst
Watch in dismay as your burnt skin transforms to ash
Listen as the Earth condemns only you for this calamity

Understand witchcraft; let it sink into your bones
Unify and become one with every charm and chant
Thoughtfully muse as you look within your soul
Carefully begin to craft your words one by one
Speak with such conviction that the air changes
Becoming dreamlike with the power of your spell
Finish your incantation with unflinching tenacity
And exhale as true magic blooms from your lips

Love Letter to a Vampire

To my most beloved immortal,

Fear not, for the moon has cycled through its many faces, and I have
emerged still loving you
Your hands are stained with carnage, your lips are wet with blood, and I
still yearn for you so
The memory of your invigorating touch jolts me awake each crisp
morning when the sun rises
The sound of your low voice floats through my head, lulling me to sleep
each dark, lonely night
Last we spoke, I expressed a deep desire to know you as intimately as a
bee knows each flower
I had asked you to write to me as soon as you could, detailing every
moment of your long life
Utterly desperate for you to describe each word you have spoken, every
dream you have dreamt
By now I have read the letter you wrote to me many times, and I have
wept over your tale of woe
And in doing so, the sky darkened at once, the air suddenly turned arid,
and the stars retreated
Almost as if even the universe could not handle hearing another word
describing such atrocities
Though the prose was filled with anguish, your love for me had miracu-
lously shone through it all
As if you wanted to give me a small sense of comfort while reading of
the horrors you endured
Even so, I long for you to be here with me, in the flesh, to wipe the
tears gushing down my face
Drag my body across wet, saturated soil, and lay me at your feet so I can
console your tired soul
Rest me atop a cloud, so I can shine down upon your frozen skin and
soothe your undead heart

If mortals knew of how you hurt, knew of the grief laced into your very skin—your very bones

They would act with less cruelty and more sympathy, and we could live a quieter life together

One filled with days as beautiful as a flourishing garden, free from judgment, drowning in love

Once, you told me that despite living eternally, you were still mystified by the meaning of life

I feel that in loving you, by allowing me so deeply into your heart, that meaning is now clear

I will always treasure your letters, your carefully written words to me, for the rest of my days

For now I know all of you, just as a bee knows each flower, just as the moon knows each star

I could sense you within the dark or hear a soft hum and know it came from your sweet mouth

I have never known another so intimately, and I feel such joy in knowing that you feel the same

Write me soon, tell me anything, tell me stories you have whispered in my ear a thousand times

I will cherish it all, memorize each stanza, every line, and stamp them upon my heart with ink

So I will never spend a day without you and your precious words beside me and within me again

Yours for today, for tomorrow, for an eternity

Creatures of the Night

Primordial tension forever remains between dusk and dawn, dark and
light
When day arrives, the sun shines innocently with pure and noble inten-
tions
Yet when midnight strikes, those intentions depart along with the
sunlight
The developing night is filled with the scent of sin and the promise of
chaos
The fates warned of times such as these, where bad omens were in
abundance
Following unsuspecting souls around like stubborn shadows, never
relenting
Singing of death and demise, of doom and destruction, of damage and
disorder

The moon closely watches over this distant world when dusk deigns to
emerge
Only when darkness spreads does the truth prevail, enthusiastically
spilling out
Secrets are revealed in spades, as plentiful as the iridescent stars within
the sky
Cruel nightmares are brought to life in the shape of viciousness and
depravity
Evil beings are exposed under the moonlight, wrapped in a dark cloak
of sin
Howls and cries and moans sound eerily like sonatas under the blanket
of dusk
Look further into the shadows; sense the monsters of the night uniting
together
Preparing to devour the tempting souls of humans straight from their
mortal flesh
Their icy kiss of death brushes upon wet lips though not firmly enough
to end
Just the right amount to invigorate, to truly experience the thrills within
the dark

Vampires gorge themselves on blood as sweet as cherry wine, as red as berries
Ghouls haunt until frightened tears fall, until eyes are soaked and lined with silver
Demons torture and torment, wielding sharp weapons of the harshest tenacity
When the naïve morning sun returns to the sky and the moon dolefully retreats
The creatures of the night dissolve once again into the cold shadows of the day
As the illusory masks and misleading lies of the light snap back into their places
Leaving no opportunity at all for the degrading depravity of the dark to reign

Part IV: Romance

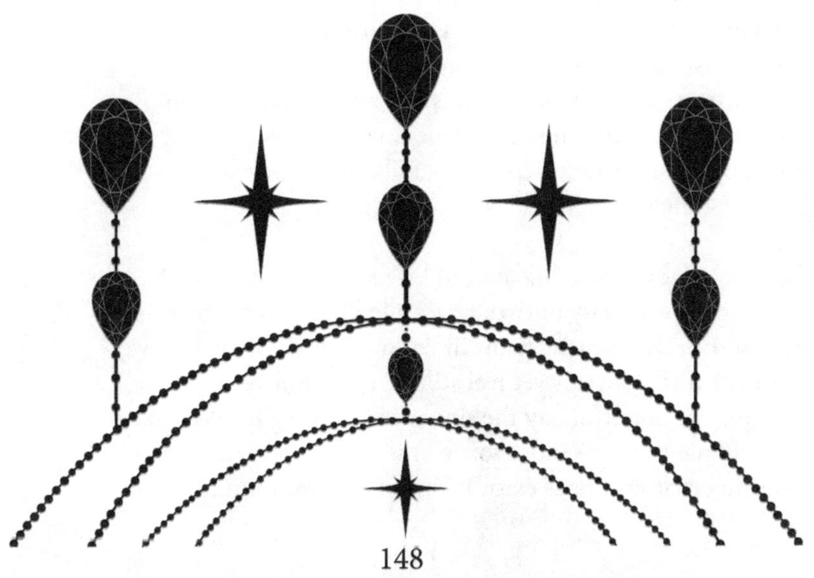

Love, Love, Love

Love: that which is a sweet myth, yet false as the rest
Altogether unattainable, unachievable, unreachable
Outstretch your arm; wrap your fist around empty air
For love only lives within woven tales of bound books
Remaining entirely elusive beyond those frail pages

Write thousands of sonnets with breathtaking passion
Pen odes and epics depicting such genuine, pure love
But it is false; it is fiction spun until others believe it
Look down at your ink-splattered palms with apathy
For you do not understand what past poets surely felt
Their lyrical words seemed full of truth, full of love
While yours seem to be empty, a void beneath them

Say the simple word again and again, *love, love, love*
Feel how bitter it tastes in your mouth, like foul fruit
Love has never touched you before, not even a graze
You would not know what it was if it nestled into you
As enigmatic as love seems, you still think of it often

Wonder what an invigorating fantasy it must feel like
For someone to look upon you as if you were a goddess
Merely visiting Earth for a time, glowing and gleaming
For someone to drink your words like a persuasive potion
One that only intensified their thirst, never quenching it
For your sensitive touch to feel like silk upon their body
Warming their dreadfully cold skin with your adoration

They say that to live a life void of love is to stifle your soul
Keeping it heartlessly buried, never allowing it to see true light
And with each moment spent in darkness, it slowly wilts away
But your soul does not yet feel stifled; it has not yet recoiled
So until the doubtful day the sky opens, shining love down
You will have to take those soft words of the poets to heart
Believing that love does exist, it simply has not found you yet

Painfully Pleasant

What if we go through life and never meet our soulmates?
Would we fall into a comfortable, calm love with another?
One filled with tedious kindness and safety and simplicity
Though knowingly missing a deeper, profound connection
Absent of the feeling that they are truly the other half of you
For love can indeed feel easy, but it does not often feel right

What if a stranger took my hand in a painfully pleasant way
In the sense that the sun sometimes shines down as a dull heat
A heat so slight, it would feel almost unperceivable on my skin
A flat sense of nothingness would then flow through my blood
I would not pull away, nor would I want to lean in any closer

Such mediocrity would feel akin to death: slow and painful
Knowing that, should I stay, a fervid love would elude me
And yet I would choose to get burned by flames in a flash
Rather than slowly drown little by little in a shallow river
So I would remove my hand from his and keep searching
For I am certain that our soulmates are somewhere out there
And their first touch upon our skin will feel anything but slight

Dream Demon

Fantasize about me; think of me; long for me
Make me your muse, your dream, your angel
Romanticize me until you think of no others
But do not fault me; do not feign such shock
When I finally reveal myself as a dark demon
I was never as good as you painted me to be
Though your portraits were always heavenly
Exposed, you now looked upon me accusingly
Until suddenly your wary expression changed
And you stared intensely into my obsidian eyes
Truly seeing me, maybe for the very first time
Stark fear or brazen desire laid within your gaze
Though I achingly prayed that it was the latter
I am not the girl you crafted within your mind
Do not blame me when you realize that at last
For that girl does not exist and she never will
She cannot cry and moan and bleed and feel
You loved a ghost, a fleeting, flickering spirit
Love me as I am instead, someone you can touch
Without your hand falling right through my flesh
Worship me; burn for me; need me; beg for me
And if you no longer dream of me each night
I will find you easily within your nightmares
I may not be the angel you believed me to be
But it is better this way; just touch me and see
Let me be your demon, baby
Will you deny me?

Never Let Me Go

Heart thundering, threatening to break free from my chest
What pleasure to feel, to know intense love, so emphatically
Innate infatuation threatens to take over and cloud my mind
Weighing down upon my fluttering eyes in a dreamy daze

If our love is untrue—nothing more than fiction—do not tell me
Keep me in this idyllic fantasy; let me bask in this perfect glow
If I am under a spell, let me worship the enchantress who cast it
Keep me unknowingly, joyfully charmed for the rest of my days

I cannot believe how lucky I am to love you, to know you
To be able to live at the same time as you, without hesitation
You loved me indefinitely and confidently, free from fear
I loved you cautiously, worryingly, plagued with concern
Always afraid the wind would blow in the wrong direction
And all of a sudden we would be devastatingly separated

I walked hurriedly into your arms, into your open embrace
Holding on closely so you would not vanish from my eyes
Hoping the spell would linger, make you never let me go
When you held me tighter, with devotion in your grip
I wept my thanks to the enchantress for making it so

Heart Strings

When April turned to May, I saw you differently
When the rain slowed and flowers began to bloom
Your mask fell and you stopped treating me kindly
The days grew scalding as your blood grew cold
Your gaze turned me to stone; your words flayed me
You touched me, and I felt more lonesome than ever
Once, you had appeared to me as an angel, but now
I had to force myself to look into your darkened eyes
And I felt as though I was with the Devil himself

Having abandoned your facade of benevolence
I began to realize how crestfallen our love made me
Drowning under the crushing depths of my misery
Suffocating from the stifling influence of your spite
I wondered if my constant tears would tint my face
Reminding me what it is like to miserably love you

With a love that would not wither away into the air
And a lover with a sharp tongue and unrelenting grip
I hung myself with the strings of your frigid heart
Strings that snapped from the weight of your malice
I could not even descend into death—a kind ending
Without you intervening, dragging me back to you
Undeniably confident I would never leave your side
And as your hold on my waist trapped me even more
I feared that might just be true

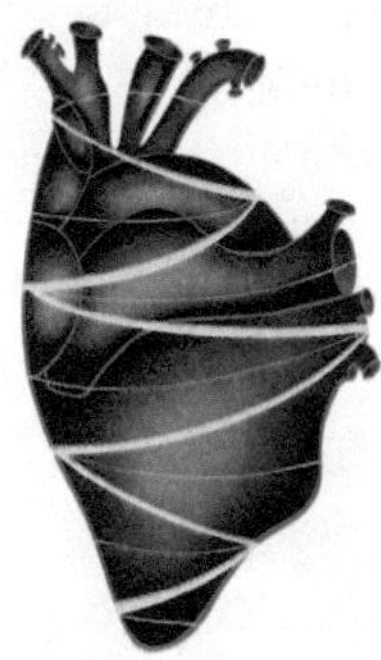

Language of Love

All of the love stories and the sentimental poems before us
Have paled in comparison to everything that I feel for you
So much so that I fear we will never be able to articulate
Just how consuming our love truly is—how exhilarating
People will never know that our affection outshines all others
And those who believe they have the greatest love story
Without a doubt will be sorely mistaken

Our love began the first time your lips parted for me
You spoke, and I was deliriously captivated by your voice
I drank your words until my body was drowning in them
For us, colloquial language seemed too inconsequential
I wished to speak the infatuated words that my soul bore
Besotted words that no one had ever gotten to hear before
Because they did not exist until the day that I met you
I wanted to craft a new language, prose meant only for us
Words that heightened our bond, spoke surely of our love
Yet covert enough that we could bask in the verses
Without inquisitive ears breaching our solitude

Although I suppose sometimes we did not need words at all
For our wanting bodies spoke of the desires within our hearts
Our skin told the story of how intimately our souls intertwined
Our bones were irreversibly branded with each other's names
As long as we remind each other of how deeply our love runs
For as long as the Earth will turn, for as long as our hearts beat
Then we can let those lesser love stories and epic poems reign
Letting them believe, foolishly, that they are as lucky as us
For as long as you are you and I am me, I will remain yours
Just as I was then, I am now, and I will always continue to be
And knowing that offers more peace than words ever could

Blood-Stained Lips

You placed a ripe raspberry between your lips, and I captured it with my mouth
Dragging it between my own lips, savoring the taste that seeped onto my tongue
Our lips were painted the color of rubies, desiring something stronger than fruit
My eyes rolled back in sensual anticipation when you reached out your hand
Letting your fingers drag over my parted lips slowly, endlessly teasing me
I swallowed the fruit as you watched my mouth move, eyes full of hunger
And I hoped, desperately, that your mouth would only crave mine tonight

Finally your mouth settled over mine and we both shuddered with passion
I gasped, entirely overwhelmed by the intoxicating, invigorating sensation
As my mouth opened further, you kissed me deeper, hungrier, as if starved
Thirsting to explore every inch, to wrap your lips around my tongue and suck
We grew more ravenous than soulless creatures, biting and piercing with fervor
Clueless that we had drawn blood until the taste settled upon both our tongues
Pulling back, we witnessed the proof of our cravings staining each other's lips
Our blood pooling, ready to drip down our faces like droplets of crimson rain
How invigorating it is to be wanted—no, to be *needed*, this passionately
Like a pair of heedless vampires who were lost in a spell of bloodlust

Blood-stained lips the very color of the fruit that we had once
indulged in
Red as fresh cherries, though the sweetness of the berries now
seemed dull
In comparison to the rich, inebriating taste of your mouth
mixed with mine
Our lips were soaking wet, saturated with blood, outright
salivating with lust
Lost to desire, we spent the rest of the night begging for an-
other taste, for *more*

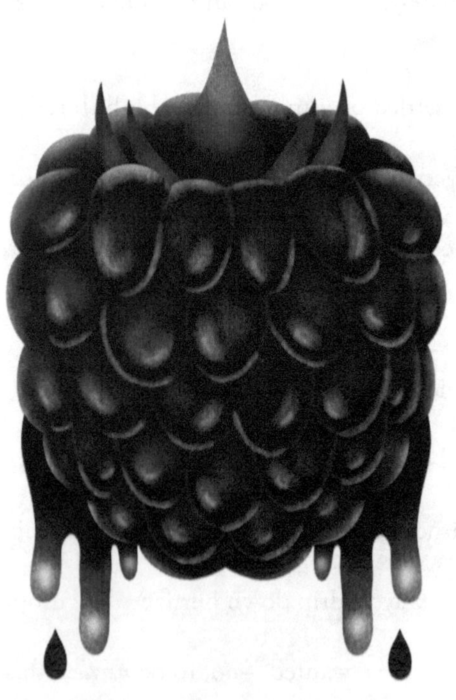

Pieces of Me

Your love for me was not true; it could not be
Not when you did not truly know me as a whole
You survived on the small pieces I offered you
I could not bear to share everything inside me
I was too worried I would become hollow

My desires and my dreams all remained a mystery
And you loved me even still, of course you did
For you did not think I had anything locked away
You thought I had given myself to you entirely
Shown you every inch of my heart, of my soul

I gave you my body, wholly and unrestrained
So you were convinced you knew my mind too
My body opened so easily for you from the start
It was the rest of me that begged to remain intact
It was my bursting mind that hoped to go unheard

You told me you loved me over and over and over
There was nothing I could do but take your hand
Hoping you would not notice how I trembled so
The burden of unspoken thoughts, bolted feelings
Preventing me from ever saying it back to you

Crush

Under an August sky I saw you as juniper and jasmine filled the air
Fate—cleverly disguised as a tumbling breeze—blew me closer to you
I knew you could feel the weight of my stare and hear my hesitant steps
Slowly turning, your green eyes, like a pair of emeralds, met mine
You walked toward me with a much more confident gait than my own
As you approached, my face heated, stained with a deep crimson hue
So dark, I was genuinely worried there would be an unrelenting mark
I could not stop blinking, trying to clear the fog clouding my mind
Trying to comprehend that you were standing directly in front of me
So near that, when you exhaled, I could feel your breath upon my lips
I inhaled sharply, no longer desiring the oxygen that surrounded me
For I wanted all of the air that I breathed to have once belonged to you
Your hand reached up to cradle my cheek, only for a fleeting moment
Before reluctantly pulling away while I averted my disappointed eyes
It was then that your hand shot back up, firmly taking hold of my chin
You boldly angled my face until I was met with your irresistible gaze
Suddenly all of the turquoise oceans and blooming gardens I had seen
Seemed bleak and insignificant in comparison to your captivating stare
You made no move to release me, content to pin me with that look
That stopped my heart for as long as I would let you, and let you I did
You spoke and I knew I would listen to your words until the sun rose
This was not yet love but something far more than mindless desire
All at once, the beginnings of a crush were then planted within us
Rooting into our souls during this sweet, scorching summer night

Déjà Vu

We were brutally and painfully separated in another life
So the gods above decided to give us this one to reunite
The people we used to be long ago somehow still remain
Lingering deeply within our souls, right alongside our pain
Awareness slowly crept up my neck; I knew I was not alone
I did not have to guess it would be you; I had already known
There you stood, as if no time had passed, not even a day
Both the same as we once were before we slipped away

Déjà vu, do you not remember me? Have we not been here before?
When you lick your lips, do you not taste me, do you not crave more?
I must have escaped your mind, your soul, though you never left mine
I begged you to think about me, your love, your heart, your valentine
But nothing sparked and nothing changed, and so I had to let you go
Yet as I put your hand in mine, one last time, your skin began to glow

Your memories gone, your mind blank, but your skin knew my skin
You longed for more, my touch ignited something so familiar within
Your body knew me; every line in your flesh stored the memory of me
Though you still could not remember, you seemed to look and truly see
Frustrated, your mind yearned to realize what your body was saying
As you gently leaned into my touch as if it was the thousandth time
Your mind gratefully started to calm, your hands soon stopped shaking
And I knew with such hope that something in your soul was close to
waking

I will spend this new life reminding you of it all
Telling you of our love, everything big and small
Even if your memories do not return right away
At least I will have you by my side, day after day

Bitter Truths

When I am sinking fast in an ocean of truly illusory, deceiving love
Force my mouth open, pour the truth down my throat until it burns
Grip my jaw; tilt my head back; more, do not stop until I am choking
Do not sweeten the words; let me taste the venomous sting of poison
Make me understand; pry my innocent eyes open; look at me deeply
Until the knowing gaze in your omniscient eyes is reflected in mine
Hold my body up when the truth threatens to wreck me completely
And kindly lay me down the moment the poison no longer fazes me

Tell me ugly, bitter truths; do not wrap a ribbon around them
Let their wicked thorns prick me until my flesh is mangled
My body will ache in agony as my mind overflows with clarity
And as the toxic truth settles into my body, and my pain ebbs
I will decide, with a newly lucid mind, to keep my mouth open
For I will now know the truth and feel impatient for more of it
Never again will I close my eyes to the harsh reality around me
And if I do, I will pry my own eyes open; I will grip my own jaw
Until my lungs are drowning in truth, never again to be deceived

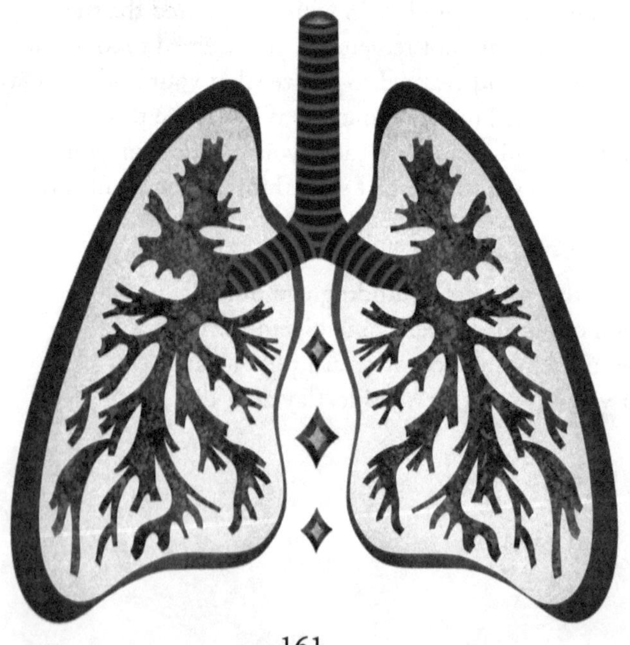

Midnight Love Potion

Craft a love potion at the stroke of midnight
Tear bouquets apart; crush fresh rose petals
Squeeze dripping nectar from sour cherries
Pour in intoxicating mouthfuls of red wine
Mix and mix and mix and mix and mix

Do not stop until the spell comes to life
Begging to take root in my open veins
Grip my jaw; force my plump lips to part
Watch me desirously drink every drop
As the concoction trickles into my lungs
Penetrating my scarlet bloodstream
Turning my body into a waiting vessel
For raw love to slide into with a gasp
Dying for dark and desperate devotion
Choking on all these evocative emotions
Yearning to feel hot, unabashed aching
Need me, want me, devour me entirely
Crave me more than the freshest water
Crawl to me until your legs are shaking
Pray to me; let me be your only religion
Sink your teeth into my trembling flesh
Then ease the pain with your wet tongue
Prove your worth with the prettiest words
Until my body is bursting with divine love

Listen as the spell speaks into the night
Whispering its words into the wind
Sanctify my body; worship at my altar
Temptingly touch me, your sacred idol
Denounce your halo; shed your wings
Become my devil; I will be your angel
But do not look upon me too closely
For even angelic souls have secrets
And mine is more demonic, hellish
Than you might ever dare to think

Searching

When she closed her eyes, she was met by a vision of a stranger
Though as he touched her, she felt a rushing sense of familiarity
She knew they had never met, yet her soul responded to his own
Like a lost lover, separated, torn apart, and now finally reunited
With an overwhelming urge to cry, she willed her tears not to fall
Blinking furiously, it was then that she looked into his own eyes
And saw they were swollen, saturated, ready to erupt, just like hers
It was a dream, yet she felt she knew his heart, just as he knew hers
She could tell that he saw right through her to her woe and worries
The stranger recognized her sorrow because he felt that sadness too
The pair sensed a magnetic pull toward the other, impossible to ignore
Two detached, disconnected halves aching to be glued back together

When they awoke, they began circling the world, looking for each other
All the while, their feet grew weary, their minds filled with hesitation
What if we spend an eternity looking, only to miss the other by a moment?
The stranger paused, then picked up his pace with a steadfast resolve
No, I must keep looking, keep searching, even if it takes my whole life
She thought the same, for their minds were as connected as their souls
And then, with her back turned from him and his back turned from her
The soulmates kept on walking away, in the exact opposite direction

Beneath the Moon

We may fall in love if we keep talking, so let us stay up all night
Cease the chill climbing up my back from the frosty evening air
By wrapping me in your embrace, shielding me from the cold
Set me on your lap, let us sit as one so I can feel your heartbeat
Whisper everything and nothing against my reddened cheek
And I will listen as if you are divulging the secrets of the world
I fell for you when you turned for a better view of the moon
I melted for you when you shifted, placing me where you stood
And murmured to me, *look, it is the perfect spot, just for you*
I gazed up, earnestly watching the moon settle amid the stars
When I turned back to your soft smile and awe-stricken eyes
I found you watching me with the worship I have for the moon
Our stares connected, and the sparkling night sky was forgotten
For everything that we could ever need and want and desire
Lies so clearly like sparkling diamonds in each other's eyes
You pressed your forehead against mine and there we stayed
Each long moment healing our tired bodies and restless minds
As the night gave way to total darkness, I climbed on your back
Letting you feel my breathing, so you know I am here; I am yours
Rain fell down upon us, the water almost glowing in the starlight
I gently closed my eyes, and you asked me where I wanted to go
Humming ever so faintly I whispered, *bring me to the moon*
And as the sky began to gleam around us, away we flew

Unrequited Love

Unrequited love is the most painful love one can endure
To want, to need, to desire, and be met with cool apathy
Is a horrid fate not even a hostile demon would sentence
With every inch of her infatuated soul, she ached for him
Eyes closed tightly, she knew she could find him in the dark
For her heart beat for him, even if his would not do the same

In the heat of summer, with passion in the air, he indulged her
And she soared idyllically, high on the ivory wings of a dove
He would smile broadly, whisper something sweet into her neck
Surely this must be true, she thought as a blush began to bloom
But as summer faded to autumn, the air turned chilly, and so did he
His fire for her seemed to have dimmed—if the flames were ever real

Her heart still tripped over itself when he appeared, her cheeks heating
Though this time, her breath caught in her throat for a different reason
Now she looked at him intently, as if no one else occupied the room
Yet he was looking elsewhere, not drawn to her presence as she was to
his
She shouted and screamed and sang, and he did not even turn to face
her

Though she now understood that her love was despondently unrequited
She could not bear to let him go, to move on, and so she grieved quietly
Weeping for what will never be, days plagued by a sense of inadequacy
Nights spent fixated, thinking of him, for if he will not love her in life
Perhaps he could love her in her dreams, and what bliss that would be

Think of Me

The air grew thick with worry around the ill-fated lovers
The couple considered themselves Romeo and Juliet
Struck by Cupid's arrow yet destined for catastrophe
Even so, knowing their tale would end in misfortune
Their love remained as unmoving as a frozen river
Oblivious or merely uninterested in the ticking clock
Counting down the seconds to their dreadful demise

Shadows told the story of their secret love
They would meet after the sun disappeared
When night emerged, wrapped in darkness
They talked and touched without hesitation
With no intention of stopping, craving more
Hoping for yet another clandestine meeting
Wanting more even before they had to part
And when the time came to tragically leave
They whispered this against each other's skin:

Whisper to me soft words I can carry with me into sleep
I will remember every last one and dream only of you
As you make my fantasies the sweetest they have ever been
Touch me tenderly; run your fingers through my hair
Kiss me in the dark, but please do not leave me yet
Not without saying goodbye, for I now need to know
That when you go out into the world, you will think of me
Just as I will think of you, every moment of every day

Their resolute devotion did not falter over the years
Perhaps because they knew they would not survive
The cost of their love, so doomed for death as it was
And love seems to be all the more potent, more urgent
When you know with certainty it will end in such loss
Still they stayed hopeful that when they meet their end
They would be able to do so together, hands intertwined
Even Death would not bear to let one live without the other
For a love so true, it would seem wicked, even for him
In this life the lovers warily hid beneath the cloak of night
Maybe they can love openly under the sunlight in the next

Obsession

He could not stop thinking of her touch, so amorous upon his skin
Her enrapturing beauty, rival to none other than Aphrodite herself
He ached for these thoughts to wither, lest they devour him whole
The sun rose and set as he fantasized, romanticizing the idea of her
She no longer existed anymore, and maybe she never truly did
For his mind warped her image into something ethereal, angelic
His lonely heart transformed into an organ impelled by romance
Capable of beating only for her, yearning to burst from his chest
So it could finally find her own heart and burrow alongside it
Both hearts beating so in sync that they would appear as one
Two hearts beating steadier than either ever could on their own

Because she fully occupied his soul, she became too much, too crushing
He longed for the gift of forgetting, the ability to erase in a gust of wind
The illusions constantly plaguing him and overpowering his senses
As if he never knew her at all, as if she had never fallen into his life
And yet whenever he tried to forget, everything within him rebelled
To never feel her phantom touch in his fantasies would be excruciating
To never imagine the warmth of her body in his mind would be tragic
His thoughts were in a frantic haze as he wailed and loved and wept
Though he could no longer remember if she was real or merely a mirage
He could not bear to exorcise her from his pining, possessed mind
So he decided to live in his fantasies, lie beside her, this angel of his
Even though he knew that one day, his love would be his demise

Cursed

The soulmates were fated to be together, for the cosmos had proclaimed it to be true
Such a bond the Fates had never seen before, and when the mates met, the Fates wept
The intensity of their heady gaze was enough to start fires, blazing with undiluted desire
The words they exchanged were filled with such immediate respect, such understanding
That the sun shone much brighter, unable to contain its delight at this exceptional pairing
In sharing a soul, they instantaneously felt complete harmony in each other's presence

They moved toward each other, both stepping at the same time, undeniably in sync
When the trio of Fates, with tears in their eyes, suddenly stepped in between the lovers
Bewildered by this intrusion, the two itched with the need to feel that the other was real
The soulmates—hands shaking, hearts racing—wondered aloud why the Fates intervened
The first Fate meekly revealed that a curse prevented the two from touching for eternity
The second Fate, softly wrapping her arms around herself, recited the curse to the mates:

A love so rare and so potent will last far more than a single moment
But one touch will be unforgiving; it will demand the life of living
You must love from afar, as though you are gazing up at a midnight star
Your love is strong; do not give into temptation and nothing will go wrong

The third Fate, drying her medley of flowing tears, begged the soulmates to heed this warning
For the curse could not be broken, not now, and not ever, though wretched and harsh as it was

The lovestruck couple, who had not broken their gaze and likely never would, considered this
They spoke through the bond in their minds, which was far stronger than any curse:

Our love will endure death; even if we spend the afterlife in a demon's arms, we will not falter
And if our touch is the cost of living, then death will greet us draped in such a loving embrace
That even the darkest demons will envy us, and cold death will not keep us apart, for if he tries
Every realm will be torn apart until we find our way back together, where we are meant to be

With that, they reached out to each other at the same time, though the Fates wailed in protest
And finally felt the heavenly touch of each other's skin; and sooner than anyone expected
The soulmates fell to the ground, still wrapped together, holding on with such reverence
Now, with unrepentant smiles upon their unmoving faces, the Fates watched them differently
With horror and delight, at this pair so in love, not even their demise could keep them apart

Forgotten Moments

My body ached for my lost love as if I was suddenly dying
Forgotten moments now abandoned somewhere within me
One morning I had awoken, and you were gone from my mind
My eyes felt empty, like someone was meant to gaze into them
I could no longer remember your taste, your touch, your scent
The lilting sound of your voice when you said that you loved me
It was all gone—you were gone—from the depths of my memory

And yet I was sure something was missing
As if I were now absent a limb or a vital organ
Though I looked and looked, inside and out
And my body remained unchanged, unharmed
I hysterically searched through my hazy mind
Though what I was meant to be looking for
I did not know; I could not recall any longer

With every day that I could not remember you
I lost more and more of myself in the process
Pieces broke off of me, and yet they lingered
Haunting me just like the fading ghost of you
Only when the memory of you returns to me
And my mind weeps with elated recollection
Only then will I once again feel complete

Indulge

Hurry, demand the most wanton pleasure for yourself
For seldom will any at all consider offering it to you
Look within; advocate for exactly what it is you need
Do not wait to be asked, for that day will not come
Listen to what your body hungers for—is starved for
And indulge greedily, with a truly ravenous appetite

Fill your desiring ears with only the sweetest sounds
Let only giving, generous hands roam over your flesh
Treat your mouth to only the ripest of delectable fruits
Wear gowns of the finest fabrics, the loveliest shades
Fall into a calming sleep; rest upon the softest pillows

In a world so dark, so very full of creatures of the night
Rampant with harrowing spirits and unbearable aching
Pleasure has the heady power to devour, consume you
And in this disturbing world, perhaps you should let it

Thief

The unsuspecting girl did not realize her lover was a vampire until it was too late
His mouth held no fangs and his heart beat just as steadily as her own
And yet, he still sucked the life from her, precisely as a creature of the dark would

Her skin became dry and cracked, her tongue dreaming of the taste of fresh, crisp water
Body trembling, shaking violently with an urgent need to collapse to the cold earth
Eyes fighting to stay open, for she knew she must stay alert, lest he take even more

In his presence, her resolve shrank, slowly enough that she did not notice at first glance
But quickly enough that one day she looked in the mirror and saw only a shell of herself
For he was drinking from her soul, from her heart, like an undead being, day after day

He became drunk from gorging himself on her, brimming with all that he did not own
The girl weakly wondered with a dying mind if he would ever feel full, wholly satiated
For she had nothing left to give to him, nothing left for him to take, to steal, to devour

As he licked his scarlet lips indulgently, for what she so hoped would be the final time
He let his eyes trail over her anguished body, now frail, emaciated, hollow in every sense
And walked away into the night, leaving her to succumb to the fatal wounds he inflicted

But the girl did not weep as she faded away into death, for she was too relieved to be alone

Heartbreak

Oh, tell me a grim story of heartbreak
One that is sure to make my soul ache
Speak to me a troubling tale of woe
Continue until my tears begin to flow

Tell me of the girl who sank to her knees in disbelief
Her love was gone, taken by the wind—a cruel thief
Tears seeped out, and an awful wailing began to start
Full of raw pain, crafted from the depths of a broken heart
She did not realize that the sounds of agony were her own
The melody was her soul grieving, emitting a miserable tone

She fell to the cold ground, grieving and hurt
And there she waited, listening beneath the dirt
Hoping to hear any sign that her love was there
Wanting to hear his voice in the frosty winter air
Maybe if she lied long enough, he would appear
Clawing through soil to wipe away just one tear
And if not, maybe the ground would take her too
She could join him and tell the earth, *thank you*

Despite her desperate pleas, her love never did rise
And the ground did not take her; it seemed unwise
So there she stayed, perpetually weeping in despair
The sound of her heartbreak still echoing in the air

Soulmates

Destined by the universe herself to be infinitely bound together
The moon softly writes the story of soulmates' love with stardust
Lightly placing the romance she has penned with such hope
Upon a cloud, hoping it will be carried gently down to Earth
Until it floats amorously through the air, waiting to be found
Hoping that soon the divided lovers will find each other too

To have a soulmate is to recognize their soul before even speaking
Words would seem trivial, for what lies within could speak for you
Silently enveloping your body, staking claim upon your very heart
Until no one else could compare, and you would not want them to

It is to have a bond that can neither be destroyed nor broken
To sever the connection—to shatter it—would be to sever your heart
Your body would survive it only scarcely, but your soul would not

It is to know one's heart so intimately that if you had to start anew
In a body void of any thoughts, any feelings, any desires or fears
And you began to slowly fill yourself up again, piece by piece
You would consist equally of their essence as you would your own

When a breeze blows by on a hot night, listen to the words it whispers
Feel a sense of solace that somewhere, someone is searching for you
With half of your split soul protected, safety sitting beside theirs
With a heart beating in anticipation, merely waiting to be loved by you
When you meet, your slashed souls will effortlessly merge back together
And the moon will then gleam, satisfied in the ending of her tender tale

Starry-Eyed Reveries

You occupy my dreams, sweetening my sleep
Lulling me even deeper into starry-eyed reveries
Moonlight casts a mystical spell over my slumber
Urging me to stay; I do not refuse; I do not want to
I weep with bliss at the thought of even more time
Spent with you inside the sanctuary of my mind
When night begins to fall, I hear your voice again
As soft as a serenade that is sung just for me
In my dreams you touch my face with such care
As if I am some sort of jewel, precious and priceless
I revel in the affectionate way you treat me, love me
Even if you are only able to do so within my mind
For a fantasy in sleep is entirely better than nothing
In the lonely light of the day

When I reluctantly awake, the dream vanishes
Yet for a moment, I remember fleeting images
Of your worshipping touch, your devout words
And I am saddened by the loss of something
Of someone whom I can no longer remember
The day moves on, slowly, in a dull, dismal haze
Though the sensation that someone is missing
Remains with a burning, lingering sort of heat
And I can do nothing but long to fall back to sleep
Waiting for the moon to graciously appear again
And the fireflies to glide radiantly through the sky
So I may close my exhausted eyes and return to you

Bruised Heart

I met you by chance in June; you left me in tears in July
I was happy just to be with you, to relish in your existence
You looked at me, and I was so grateful for the attention
That I did not realize there was little love left in your eyes

You felt like a dream, so sweet, tasting just like summer
That I did not realize how my insides incessantly hurt
From the bitterness of your touch seeping into my flesh

I felt like a warm body to you, so soft, so willing, so available
I was thrilled to let you have my body however you wanted
If I could have even the slightest piece of your heart in return

Instead you took my body, my heart, my happiness
As I brought my tongue to my lips, I no longer tasted summer
Only the flavor of an icy winter night lingering in my mouth

You never deserved to feel my skin, to glory in it as you did
And I shrink to think of the mark that you left on my heart
You can keep my bruised heart, for I will grow a new one
And I will keep it better protected from those just like you

Labor

Sweating from the labor of loving you
Amorously killing myself to serve you
My body breaks from your demands
My hands struggle from supporting you
Oh, what straining work it is to be yours

To belong to you is taxing and tiring
For you expect too much out of me
I cannot be your moon and your sun
I cannot be everything to you, for you
And as I falter, you do not realize why

Break me if you must; I am already ruined
Stick your fingers down my tender throat
Watch as I do not gag, as I do not flinch
I am used to you forcing things upon me
For I have grown complacent to survive

With a mind that has shut down entirely
To protect itself from all you have done
And with a body that longs to captivate
But only pacifies, too sore to fight back
The tiring exertion of our—of *your*—love
Has finally laid me down upon the floor
Here I stay, hopefully far away from you

Pleading

How can God exist if he made someone as thoughtless as you?
You find my bruises and press in until I am wailing with agony
My throat bares your marks, strangled until I beg for breath
You lick the tears falling from my swollen eyes, savoring the taste
You lay me down upon a star, the brightest one, almost blinding
Its sharp edges cut into my skin, and blood begins to drip, slowly
Traveling from my naked throat down to my shivering legs
Every time I try to move, to escape, the star wounds me further
Until I pray, pleading for you to let me down and notice my agony
Imploring you to see the blood furiously running down my flesh
You slowly turn—reluctantly—and look at my distraught face
But remain oblivious to the palpable hurt etched in my skin
My despairing eyes, my rapidly falling tears, my flushed cheeks
I am sure you imagine I am crying out of gratefulness to you
How kind it is that you brought me here, all the way to the sky
How could I ever be in any sort of pain after such a caring gesture
You bear no sympathy for the excruciating pain plaguing my heart
And my body is left to writhe in horrific devastation in return

Leaving

There is nothing I could do to make you stay
I would never attempt to shackle you to my body
For I would lose a vital part of myself in the process
Better for you to leave now, while my heart is intact
For if I ever began to beg you to stay by my side
My heart would continue to give itself over to you
You would have shards of a heart you do not want
And I would be absent of a heart that has failed me

Your mind was locked; I could not find the key
I would not break the door or tear off the hinges
Not when you did not strongly urge me to do so
There was nothing I could do to guide you back
I could not make you see if you refused to look
If you shut your eyes from the world—from me

Help, exorcise me from you, *please, please*
For I will not be strong enough to do it myself
Forget my voice; blur my face; erase my touch
Let me exist in a world where we have never met
For the memory of you leaving is too much to bear

I love you enough to never see you again
If I must stay in this world, in this body
I know that you will tirelessly haunt me
For you have invaded my heart, my soul
And that will have to be enough, for now

Reunited

Maybe it is so difficult to find your true soulmate
Because your soul does not fully remember theirs
It reacts, feeling an intense pull upon first meeting
But wariness holds your soul back from truly trusting
It is when you fully learn what they store in their heart
When you realize you cannot go a day without them
It is then that your soul will ardently remember

When your souls are back together, they rejoice at once
Reunited after being unwillingly separated in another life
Molding together instantly, never again wanting to be apart
That is when you know you have found your true soulmate
When you let every part of your other half in so completely
Your body readjusting to accommodate the space they need
And instead of feeling overwhelmed at the intrusion
You finally feel whole, able to feel absolute harmony

In hindsight you were irrevocably theirs, just as they were yours
The world twisted, rearranged itself so you would find each other
Knowing with certainty that once you were within each other's sight
You would never want to look elsewhere again, and you never did
Maybe you met in a past life, living and loving until the very end
And when you started over, as different people in different places
You still found your way back to each other, as soulmates always do

Bloom

All at once I began to feel
The clouds shuffled slightly
Letting the sun filter through
Something inside of me changed
The possibility of love was planted
And with it, I began to flourish

Cut me open; watch my veins bleed roses
Gaze at the stars swirling in my bright eyes
Hear my full heart singing Cupid's song
Feel the frigid exterior of my skin shed
Romance now flows through my blood
Bursting at the seams, trying to escape
I want to bathe in it and swallow it greedily
Hoping to experience love in such excess
That it might be considered truly sinful
I can feel love within my eager grasp
As my fingers graze something sweet
Wonderfully divine, I savor the touch
Waiting and waiting, biding my time
Until the touch becomes an embrace
One I will never imagine parting from
Never again do I close my tired eyes
Never again do I fall into a deep sleep
Worry and terror constantly fill me
Thinking love will fade back into an idea
A myth of fabricated tales, clever lies
That it will disappear into the night
Silently float away in a gust of wind

Weak with exhaustion, eyes watering
I sense the roses still under my skin
And feel my worry start to dwindle
Soon I know love will hold me
And I will finally, fully bloom

Ravage and Ruin

Pine for me; ache for me; beg for me, just as I would do for you
I long for you to choke me and wrap your hands around my throat
Possessively, so I may lay my hands over yours, pushing down
Press harder; give me a head rush; make me lightheaded from lust
Do not stop until I am shivering, cold and hot, pleading for more
Ravage me; ruin my shuddering body until I am no longer aching
Encase the room in darkness; bind my wrists with silken fabric
The soft material barely creating friction against my bound hands
My flesh will yearn for you to tie me even tighter, even rougher
Until I can feel a sharp sting from the unforgiving, taut restriction
Make me writhe beneath you, squirming, pulling at the restraints
Though in truth, I would have no true desire to break free from you
For your pheromones ignite something incendiary within me
Glide your hands attentively, unhurriedly, across my collarbone
Watch as goosebumps materialize beneath your expert touch
Touch me until my skin is laden with your dominating marks
Until it is rife with the prints of your fingers digging into my skin
Restraints or not, I would know that I was already bound to you
And as the fabric would embed into my skin, I would tell you so
Your desire would be mine, just as my pleasure would be yours
We would greedily indulge each other, with no signs of stopping

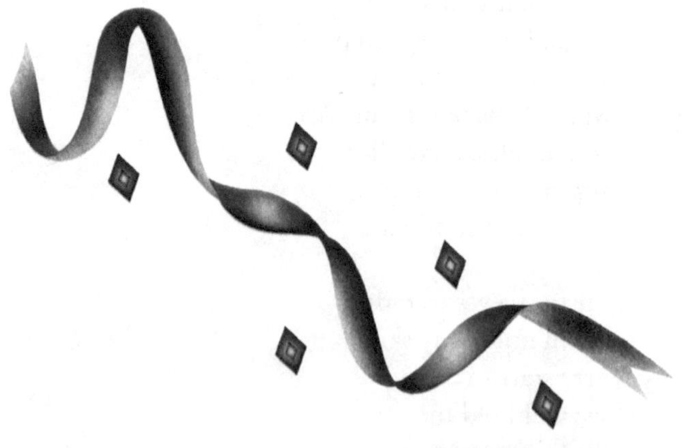

Beware

Wait, distance yourself from loving romance
Just for a moment, just to take a deep breath
Remember that not all love is honest, sincere
That love does not keep the world spinning
So do not give it a power it does not deserve
Love can be cruelly caustic and destructive
Just as it may be magical and breathtaking

Love does not feed the soil on the earth
It does not help the flowers to flourish
Love will not stop a drought in a desert
It will not make rain fall from the sky

Love is not anything and everything
Look elsewhere for joy and for peace
For love can disappear into the night
Leaving, before you open your eyes

Love will hide spite within pots of sugar
Open the locked jars before it is too late
Love can blind and break into fragments
Beware, or it just might break you too

Be careful to keep your eyes wide open
Trust with caution and with attentiveness
For a love without the purest of intentions
Can be so crushing you may never recover

Doubt

Feel a raindrop of doubt and know that a mist of dread is close behind
Look up, no, higher; see the rain pouring down; it is inescapable now
Let the storm wash over your mind and body like a towering tide
Feel the acidic sting of the water on your skin and open your eyes

Realize that their own eyes are cold and unfeeling
So full of darkness, they hold no ounce of affection
Notice that their cloying blood is so tainted, polluted
Even buzzing mosquitoes do not desire to touch them
Open up their ice-cold veins; wonder what lies within
Watch heaps of black tar pour out, thick with sadism
Look into their bitter soul, so very sickening and rotten
That even the freshest fruit turns sour upon their lips

Your soft sweetness diminishes, dissolves, as their malevolence grows
As if your innate goodness acts as kinder to the hot flames within them
Perpetually burning around their unloving heart—if they have one at all
And though their true nature is revealed, you cannot bear to let them go

Seemingly ambrosial, as sugary as golden molasses
Their masqueraded love still drips down your body
Seeping into your waiting, unknowing bloodstream
Saccharine sap slowly turns to acid within your veins
Though you shouldn't, you embrace it all the same
Even fatal poison spewed from their mouth is better
Than gleaming gold from the hands of someone new
Suck the venom out only when you fall to the ground
Lifeless, yet your broken heart still beats for them
Though you are shrouded in stark sadness, so genuine
Soon their deadly toxins will turn back into molasses
And it will have all been just a dizzying dream, right?

Eclipsed

Everything grew different the day you met her
Though I was a bright star, she was the sun
And she would always eclipse me in your eyes
You gazed at her with such awe and admiration
While you glanced at me with quiet indifference
Even if I were to transform into a shooting star
Flying fiercely, twirling across the twilight sky
Your eyes would be intently fixed on the sun
When she falls away into the night, dim and soft
You will gawk at her with the sharp stare of love
What if I became the moon, the sun's counterpart
Just as luminous but glistening in a different way
Would you suddenly tumble into a deep slumber
Missing my entrance only by a few scant seconds
Impatient to not have to witness my gleaming tears
For vivid as I would be, my heart would still ache
Yet maybe it would not matter at all who I became
For I knew I could suddenly transform into the sun
And you would swiftly decide you prefer the stars

Illicit

Forbidden love—no, forbidden lust, captured us in her reckless grip
We never harbored any great affection nor true admiration for the other
Simply a deep-seated feeling of desire burned within both of our bodies
Eclipsing lustful thoughts of all others who now paled in comparison

Our arctic hearts did not beat to the tune of romance
I did not long to craft perfect poetry about your lips
You did not try to pen sonnets about my hazel eyes
And still, even when we had not yet fallen prey to love
Even when we flew solely on the wings of carnal lust
We were still forbidden to indulge in these sensual desires
Never allowed to touch, for ruin would rain down upon us
If we risked acting upon our uncontrolled passions
Our attraction was utterly forbidden, fated for disaster
And yet we still held on to the cravings of our bodies
And let them shine through our passionate eyes
Letting our gazes find each other, only for a moment
Though something so innocent still set my body alight
Reaching up, I placed my hand on the nape of my neck
Wishing I was in your grasp, my skin beneath your touch
You indecently hooked your thumb into your bottom lip
Pulling down slightly, wishing that your hand was mine

Toeing a line we were not allowed to cross
We continued on with this illicit affair of ours
Stealing brief seconds like thieves in the night
Until our fleeting looks were soon not enough
And we decided to welcome the chaos as one
As we promptly reached out like we never had
And gave into the commands of our yearning
Destruction immediately surrounded us both
But we were already too consumed in our lust
To spare the damage even a momentary glance
For even though the world was entirely on fire
We too were sheathed in such fervent flames
From the scorching heat of our inescapable touch

Blissfully Bound

I give my love to you willingly but do not feel empty
You give and give in return, and I feel fuller than before
Love should not feel like a sacrifice, a detrimental loss
It should be an offering: to give and never think to take

Unravel me like a spool of thread; I beg of you
Do not stop until I am laid bare, every inch untangled
Place my strings around your body again and again
Until we are beautifully and blissfully bound as one

Intertwined, a moment with you can feel like a lifetime
If I was gifted immortality, I would scream with delight
Glad to be freed from the constricting confines of time
With anyone else, it would be a curse of the worst kind
Hexed to live a monotonous coexistence, bleak and dreary
With you, it would feel like the angelic kiss of a saint
For an eternity can feel like heaven within the right arms

We would live happily for the rest of our undying lives
Filled to the brim with love, faces creased with passion
Evermore tied tightly together by an unbreakable thread
Two bodies fused as one, as we were always meant to be

Enemies

Cycles of riveting rumors and gossip stood between a sweet girl and a
wicked boy
Their animosity had been fueled by misperceptions rife with such cruel
accusations
The wicked boy was arrogant at his very core, heartless, and ravenous
for authority
He was told she admonished his conceit, thinking him to be as vicious
as a villain
The sweet girl was selfless, thoughtful, and her heart beat only to the
tune of peace
She was informed he viewed her altruism as weakness, as feeble as a
meek maiden

And yet, unbeknownst to the other, neither had taken part voicing these
harsh words
It was the work of others, buzzing around them as bees, planting these
lies as truths
Until their eyes were covered in a mist of deceit they could not seem to
cut through

Whenever their gazes locked, the flickering tension in the air grew
tenfold
The pair would watch each other closely with a stoic mask of fury on
their faces
Though as time passed, the haze lifted—only slightly—and things
began to change
They suddenly crossed paths more often than normal, and the air
seemed to soften
Secretly they hoped the rumors were false, for they always felt drawn to
one another
Both ravenous to truly know the person behind the gossip floating
within their minds
He did not loathe her quiet nature, and she did not flinch from his
assertive aura

And so, with a subtle nod of his head, he beckoned her toward a dimly
lit hallway
To which she wasted no time following in his direction, until merciful-
ly, finally
The supposed enemies found themselves truly alone for the very first
time

They spoke until their throats were hoarse, mouths dry, feeling a sudden
longing to stay
They dispelled false narratives spun by those with thoughtless hearts and
sinful minds
The ice that had once filled their eyes in a glacial look of hostility had
now melted
Burnt up by a voracious, feverish sort of heat that neither of them knew
what to think of

What they did know was that the longer they spoke honest truths
straight from their core
And the longer they stood with their bodies mere inches away from
touching one another
They knew, that they were enemies no longer, if they had ever truly
been from the start
The sweet girl and the wicked boy stayed in that hallway until the lights
fully faded
And though darkness surrounded them, their eyes had never before
been more clear

One Thousand Letters

I have written you one thousand letters that you will never read
And I will write you one thousand more as love guides my hand
Simply knowing that all my thoughts about you, to you, for you
Are written down, seeped in ink, and fondly placed on paper
Is enough to bring me some peace, at least for a little while

My words will dotingly speak of our near perfect love story
The way I felt inside when you looked at me the day we met
With such blushing charm and warm worship in a single gaze
How the universe shook and shifted when you finally touched me
Gently, as if you were worried your hands would slip right through

My letters will remind you of your constant, tender words to me
Spoken against my lips, telling me how I have always been yours
They will remind you that my soul avidly pines for you even still
For though you may not be in my life, you still remain in my heart

Maybe we can be together in the next life or the one after that
We could even be stars in the sky, sparkling together endlessly
Or maybe someday soon the wind will speak my words to you
And you will brighten, listening closely, intently, reverentially

But until then I will carry on writing and waiting with devotion
For as long I think of you with fondness, not a day will pass by
When I do not rapidly reach for a pen, ready to write once more

Eyes

Mystified by the brazen look in your eyes
Dizzy with a strong sense of anticipation
My blood buzzed whenever you were near
A chorus of bluebirds sang mellow melodies
Burrowing deep into my besotted bones
Slipping through my shuddering fingers
Buried further into my infatuated mind
Every time we crossed paths by chance
My soul became more and more stained
With thoughts of you, feelings for you
Each time we parted ways far too quickly
I worried that we would never reunite
I spent my cloudy days hearing your words
Echoing in my ears, like the sweetest music
I spent my cold nights musing poetically
About your hand buried deep in my hair
Pulling, angling my head to look up at you
Meeting your gaze of desire and admiration
I could draw you perfectly, even blindfolded
For I still see you with perfectly sharp clarity
Within the shadowed corners of my mind
Underneath my skin you thankfully remain
And I only wish for you to say the same
Next time we are together, I merely yearn
For you to look upon me for so very long
That when you close your eyes to sleep
You will see me imprinted in your vision
Like when you stare at the sun for too long
And her iridescent luminosity stays with you
Let me be your ghost, one that does not haunt
A spirit that lives in the crevices of your mind
Admiring each thought you invoke and conjure
Holding dearly onto every word that you speak
Although you do not need to say anything at all
For I could merely gaze into your bright eyes
And know everything I would ever need to

Wilting

Scoop the sweet nectar from the honeycomb that is my body
Keep going, even more, further, until I am but an empty shell
Sticky and raw with the remnants of whom I once used to be
The sounds of my futile desperation echoing in such despair
Hauntingly bouncing off the walls of my now bare skeleton
I am empty, full of darkness, existing as nothing and no one
My lips part, trying to speak, but the words come out sour
My hands had once felt as if they were crafted by silkworms
But now they have changed, becoming as callous as a boulder
While the warmth of my heart has turned cold and unmoving

As you bring *my* saccharine syrup to your lips
Feel it coat your tongue and inundate your lungs
Filling your vacant body to the brim with *my* life
Your voice now sounds sugary, just like molasses
Your abrasive skin now feels sinfully smooth, soft
Your soul has bloomed into an affectionate flower
Offering its sickly-sweet sap to anyone but me
You have flourished from the contents of *my* soul
While I have silently wilted away to nothing at all

Betrayal

Your betrayal hurt with staggering force
Your duplicity robbed me of my breath
But beyond the betrayal, beyond the lies
What hurt the most, what made me weep
Was when you stopped looking upon me
As if I was the only person who existed
The only one in the world that mattered
That is when I burst, silently screaming

Once, you were my only source of heat
And now I will feel permanently frigid
Forever shivering, without you beside me
I had never felt so entirely deserted, so alone
And the one person I most wanted to talk to
About my pain, about everything, was you
And that thought fully shattered me whole
Breaking me more than I thought possible

Flames of Love

Deep breaths and cigarettes, little deaths and clear regrets
Our love was ready to combust, on the verge of demise
Drunk on wine and hope, I hesitantly stayed and waited
As our love, once blithe and airy, became asphyxiating

I grew weak as you stood tall, telling me lingering lies
You told me I was your lighter, I ignited the fire in you
I stood by, watching the flames quickly moving closer
As I was burned, you asked me to stay and reignite you
I was in a mindless haze with smoke clouding my mind
Trying to leave, the sounds of my choking filled the air
Coughing so severely, I thought I might deposit a lung
You merely scoffed, fixing me with such a callous look
That I knew I could not leave, shackled by invisible chains
Vacantly watching the flames slowly extinguish around me
But knowing that soon I would have to light you up again
And with that thought, my panting lungs recoiled at once

Our love is sure to end me, for you will not hear my pleas
And as your fire singes my body to the ground, you will leave me
My ashes will seep into the dirt, grateful to be freed from this life
Our love, at last, will be over, and hopefully, in the soil I will stay
Never again to feel the cruel flames of love seize my tired soul

Lust

Lovely, lovely lust
It feels like crimson cherry juice
Dripping so seductively down my lips
Sucking, moaning around a cherry pit
Hollowing out my cheeks with hunger
Tying a cherry stem with my tongue
Moving with slow, careful precision
Pleased in the way you watch me
Mouth watering and hands shaking
With the manic need to touch me

Lingering, lingering lust
It feels like an angel upon your skin
Teasing touches to put you in a trance
And it sounds like a devil rasping to you
Sending chills throughout your body
Hiding from the revealing light of day
Waiting for nighttime to come at last
So it can slink through the darkness
And latch onto aching, writhing flesh

Longing, longing lust
It feels like the culmination
Of every glance, every touch
All the yearning and wanting
Begging to come to fruition
Quivering and trembling so
Give into your reckless desires
Revel in the way lust consumes
With such an insatiable hunger
Never deny yourself the pleasure
That lust promises to deliver

Skeleton

Tell me you love me when you want me beyond my body
And do not dare to speak the words even a moment sooner
Want me in your heart before you ever desire me in your bed
Crave my body only after you crave my mind, my intellect
Do you even realize that I have a mind, a brain of my own?

When I ventured to question what you loved the most about me
You responded instantly with, *your hips, your hair, your mouth*
And I knew that you did not know me—love me—as I believed
You never saw the poison in my veins slowly stealing my life
You were too busy trying to touch me again and again
I was drowning, choking, and all you did was turn away
I was dying day by day, and you only aided me in disappearing

I wonder if when my body is no longer at your fanatical disposal
If you will finally miss me when your eager hands are empty
For my warm flesh—something you can place your cold lips upon
Is the only thing that could ever make you beg me to come back
I worry you like my mouth because of what it does for you
Rather than what it could say, what it so earnestly wants to say
Even if I spoke, you would not listen to the words spilling out
Your eyes would be too fixed on the way my lips were moving
My words are deemed empty and trifling, but that does not matter
As long as my pouty lips are parted and my tongue is wet enough

If I became the sun, you would grow irate as my skin scalded
Because your hands could not withstand the heat I was enduring
If I became the moon, you would grow angry at my vast distance
Because my body would not be within reach of your hungry touch
Love me as a skeleton, void of soft skin, heart-shaped lips, silky hair
Or do not bother to love me at all

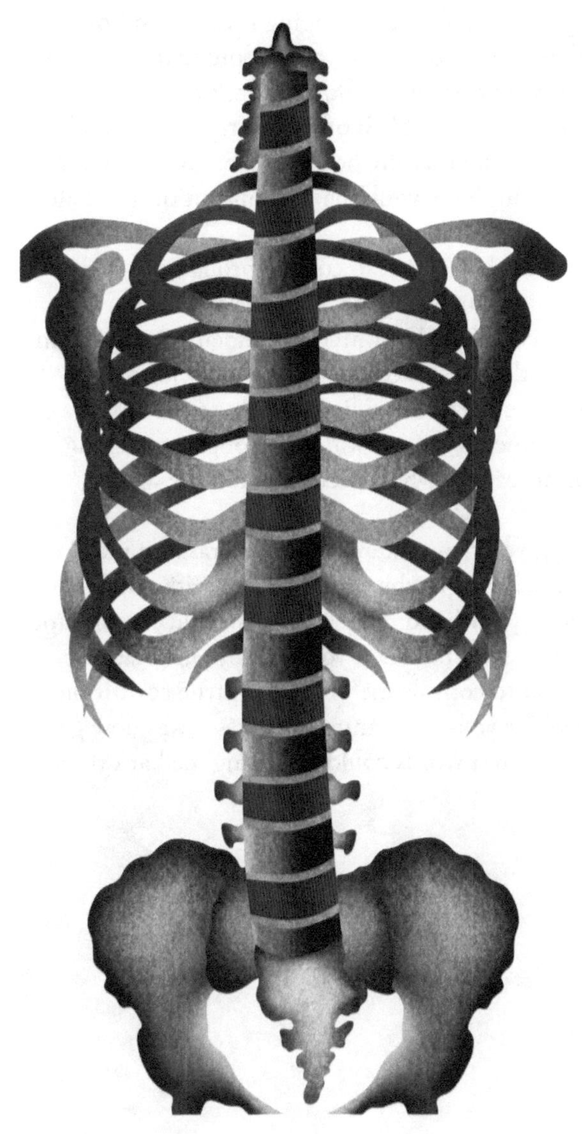

Falling

I tumbled out of love slowly, much slower than I fell into it
It happened gradually, like sand slipping through an hourglass
Each grain embodied another part of my soul that you stole
Pieces that I fiercely wished I could take back from you
You held too much; you held all of my heart in your hands
You held on so harshly that my bones broke; my blood burst
And I worried soon there would be nothing left of me at all

The sound of your desire used to course through my body
As you moaned into my ear, your words seemed so sweet
That I did not yet realize the contempt hidden beneath them
Eventually, even the most saccharine tones on your tongue
Could not disguise the derision lining your every word
And your light touches on my skin grew rough, punishing
Though I was never sure what exactly I had done wrong

The scorn lining your soul intensified your grasp on me
And my pleasure began to ebb, mind cloudy with confusion
I tried to wrench your hands from my wrists, but I could not
You would not relent, and when you saw my sincere panic
And did not rush to console me or act with true contrition
I knew my love for you—as waning as it was—was now gone
And even the sweetest words could not bring me back to you

Fireheart

My cold heart was set entirely on fire upon meeting you
I was worried my skin would char, my bones would melt
My body was ablaze from the flames burning in your eyes
From one look I could almost feel the weight of your touch
As if your lips and tongue were unabashedly moving over me
You pressed your mouth to mine, inciting a firestorm within
Dizzy, I licked my lips in a stunned trance and tasted smoke
Twin flames, two bodies, one soul so desperately searching
Aching to be reunited, dreading the moment they must part

When the universe tore us in two, I found my way back to you
Because your heart is wholly mine, and mine is wholly yours
I found you far before your mouth ever opened to call to me
For your fear bled into my mouth until all I tasted were ashes
And only when our gazes reunited and my hand was in yours
Did the embers of our separation vanish, replaced by flames
For our hearts are furnaces, waiting to burn any tendrils of fear
Waiting to scorch anything that is not the love we both cherish

My own light grew dark when I did not have you beside me
The further away you walked, the more I felt the fire in me fade away
I held the match but could not yet summon the strength to set it aflame
When you returned to me, you did not give me the blistering gift of
heat
Nor did you take it upon yourself to provide me the light that I needed
You simply stood close until I felt your warmth seeping into my bones
Looking at me with such care, such certainty in the power of our bond
Finally I let myself take in the silent words laced into your deep gaze
Feeling the darkness in my body now give way to warm, soothing light
Until all at once I began to burn at last, sheathed in a lovesick inferno

My fireheart, my soul, light me on fire with the embers of your love
And I will wrap the flames around my heart, eternally, everlastingly

Teasing

I could not resist you any longer, body tense, filled with such desire
Moving closer toward you even though the ground was ablaze with fire
My fingertips itched to reach out, to know what your skin felt like
I would withstand hell if I could experience heaven in your hands
If only for a few breathtaking, heart-pounding moments of ecstasy

As you moved closer, you touched me so lightly, not enough to satisfy
But enough to incite a burning heat that crawled through my aching
body
You traced patterns on my skin, and when you saw my goosebumps
Your hands gently settled upon my thighs, trailing upwards, teasing
Moving so slowly, I thought I might faint from my spreading need

Your taunting touches grew bolder and bolder, leaving me breathless
As you gathered my hair in your hands and wrapped it around your fist
I moaned as your mouth and tongue traced a wet line down my throat
Your lips moved over my racing, erratic pulse, and I almost wept
Captivated by impious lust, I was overtaken by your every touch
Glad you held me closely, for I could not imagine staying upright
The moment when you decided to finally press your lips against mine

Next Love

The next person to love me will do so selflessly, generously
He will worship my name, begging to know me intimately
Wasting no time learning the taste of every inch of my skin
For he will not stand any part of my body to go unloved
He will treat my heart and mind with the same rapt attention
And impassioned dedication that he bestows upon my skin
I will feel so loved that happiness will waft off of me amply
People passing by on the street will beg for me to perfume it
He will tell me he would live a thousand lifetimes with me
Even if I decided to never let him touch my skin again

Thick tears will stream shamelessly down his sweet face
When I tell him I love him for the very first time
He will cherish me and care for me like no other before
I will rejoice that all my past loves and heartbreaks
Have given me so much room to cultivate this new love
A love that has my heart bursting, breaking at the seams
Heaving with respect and passion, admiration and trust
And such kindness that I never knew existed before
I will ask, bashfully, for only a sliver of his heart
Without hesitation, he will reach deep into his chest
Pull out his wet, beating heart, and place it in my palms
Saying he would give me the world if only I ever asked
And with such pure love in his voice, I will believe him

Free

Cut my hand on piercing shards of broken glass
Watched my blood pour out like opulent wine
Hoping my love for you would flow out too
Making no move at all to staunch the bleeding
With no desire to stitch up the horrid wound
And though I felt lightheaded from the pain
A sense of calmness began to wash over me
Suddenly my constricted heart was light again
I felt astonishingly relieved, unrestricted, free
Before me sat a puddle of who I used to be
The person I became when I loved you
And I was glad to go back to my true self now
To leave you behind, utterly lost to my past
It was then that my once gory cut healed
Not even leaving behind a scar on my skin
I let go of you entirely and rejoiced
Finally, I thought, *I can breathe*

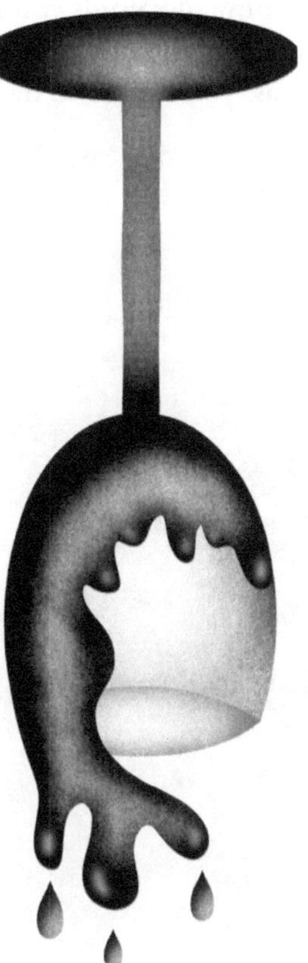

Alone

Beyond the heartfelt, genuine warmth of love and romance
And past the poisonous pain of heartbreak and deception
You are left only with yourself: a skeleton forced to live
Straining to crawl through this long life in silent solitude
When the unforgiving sun sets and the frigid moon rises
Only the agonies ingrained within can keep you company
Though it is tiring to walk through life with an empty hand
It is also freeing to live for yourself and focus on reflection
To look within your heart and know that it beats only for you
Without the burden of love, for whether it is sweet or rotten
It is a liability all the same, weighing on your very soul
Without that affliction, exhale in delight at the empty space
That now surrounds you night after night in tranquility
Though you may be living, heaving through life with woe
At least you can do so by yourself, mercifully all alone

Part V: Reflection

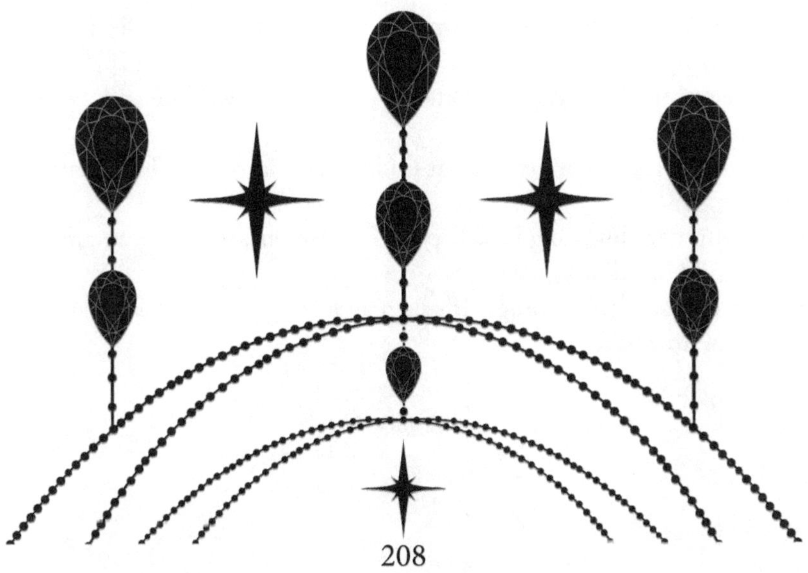

Cauldron

She was crafted in a cauldron, born of oranges and marigolds and everything bright
Dripping wet, smelling of citrus and cinnamon, golden hair like sunlight, she emerged
Frightened, she looked down upon her body, created solely for the pleasure of others
Feeling revolted, noticing her supple skin their brusque hands will soon touch and take
Tempted to chop off her smooth hair their hands will wrap around, forcefully pulling
Nauseated by her sultry lips their hungry mouths will indulge in over and over again
She wanted to admire her beautiful body, but it only reminded her of a future too ugly

Scared, close to shaking though she stood tall, meeting the gaze of every man nearby
Men that spelled her with evil intent, now leering, eager to mold her to their own will
Eyes black with wickedness and void of any fear, for how could they ever understand it
When they were not born as a woman in a world rife with vile and domineering men
But the girl from the cauldron knows—she knows we enter this world in such shame
Tears are spilled at her arrival, but underneath lies a sort of infuriating pity from all
Pity from men, knowing how they will destroy us, thinking we are meek, mild, modest
Pity from women, knowing with such agonizing certainty what we will come to endure

She was sweet and sugary and syrupy, but under the sap something sinister remained
Something the men did not see, for they were too busy cheering at their perfect creation
Knuckles white with anticipation, they did not see the fortitude within her sparkling eyes
She was made for men, but she knew even now that she would never kneel before them
She would sooner return to the walls of the cauldron than feel the touch of a man in lust
She was golden and gleaming and glowing, and she would blind them all with her beauty
Until the last thing they ever saw was her tempting body walking far, far away from them

Woman

Open your weary eyes and let yourself weep
It takes so much effort to just *exist* as a woman
Fighting every single day to be seen, to be heard
Only to be reduced down to the color of our hair
The feel of our lips, and the shape of our bodies
Women are everything except who we want to be
We live but always for others, never for ourselves

To be a woman is to suffer, to agonize in silence
Our tears are bitterly forced back into our eyes
Our screams of frustration stuck in our throats
Our rage is blaring within, begging to be released
Fury eternally coats our hearts, lines our lungs
Begging anyone who will listen to be freed

Hatred blooms in the sore stomachs of women
Loathing from being forgotten and ignored
Such grief and misery will continue on unknown
Our pain will go as undetected as a silent wraith
Not even the walls will whisper of how we ache
Maybe one day, we too will become ghosts
Though maybe as women, we already are

Blame

Women are born with blame placed upon us
As though we have done something wrong
Just by entering and existing in this world
Blame lingers like a relentless branding
And our souls feel utterly weighed down
By the apparent burdens we seem to be
When we are thrust into a perfect garden
And witness a weed emerging, we wail

Irrefutably we willed that weed to sprout
For we are at fault; we always have been
I am so sorry, we will confess to the flowers
Though we do not have any idea for what
Only that the garden, completely innocent
Has been tainted by our very presence
And for that, we must begin to atone
We are born swaddled in accusation
And we will die wallowing in guilt

Ache

Knead your heart with your palm; soothe an ache you cannot place
Then turn and look at her; see the woman who is being followed home
Wrapping her arms around herself as she is closely stalked in the dark
Picking up her pace—but not too fast—willing her tears to stop falling
Look into her devastated eyes; see your own sadness reflected in them
Oh, you think to yourself, *I understand now*, for you do not know her
But you know her pain; you know that her fear is so horribly familiar
You can still taste it on your tongue and feel your heart stutter in reply
The discomfort is even worse now and you wonder if it will ever relent
As the woman continues to be watched by evil shadows with evil hands
You think to yourself, *no, the pain will not fade, not now, and not ever*
So keep kneading your heart, soothing an ache you know all too well
Wishing that you could walk alone at night, with only the dark to fear

Origami Rose

When women say we feel suffocated, this is what we mean:
Agreeing with others to make them all feel more in control
Being silent, wholly soundless, so everyone else may speak
Letting all others perceive us as weak, as gullible, as naïve
Bending and twisting so everyone will have an easier path
Submitting and shrinking so everyone will have more space
Belittling our own thoughts, our secret dreams, our desires
Holding our breath with expert ease when others are around
Feeling ashamed, almost embarrassed, by our need for oxygen
The air was put there for others, though never for ourselves
Our bodies somehow never seem flat enough, small enough
Subconsciously trying to seem more compact, compressed
Folding ourselves up and over and in, like an origami rose
Exquisite, though cautious never to take up too much space
And there we stay, folded up and tossed aside without care
Until we realize we cannot breathe, for the scraps of oxygen
We meekly breathed in have proven to be not enough to live
Gasping now, silently trying to unfold our crumpled bodies
Just enough to wordlessly inhale, and as we modestly do so
We spend the whole time hoping we are not taking too much

Bitten Tongues

We learn to censor ourselves so early
Bite our tongues; swallow our words
It is intrinsically established within us
Until being silent is all we know to do

We worry when we open our mouths
When we boldly risk speaking aloud
Our soft, innocent words will be taken
Turned into something fierce and sharp
Others will quickly claim to be sliced
Carved open from our virulent malice
So we sew and stitch our lips closed
Until our words remain only our own
Freely grown within our weary minds
Plucked from our tired, haunted souls
They exist only for ourselves, for now

Maybe one day our voices will be heard
Our thoughts will seep from our pores
Implanting right into the minds of others
Without needing to open our mouths
Our words will be seen for what they are
And be received with true understanding
We will effortlessly pry open our mouths
Unclench our jaws and tongues, and speak

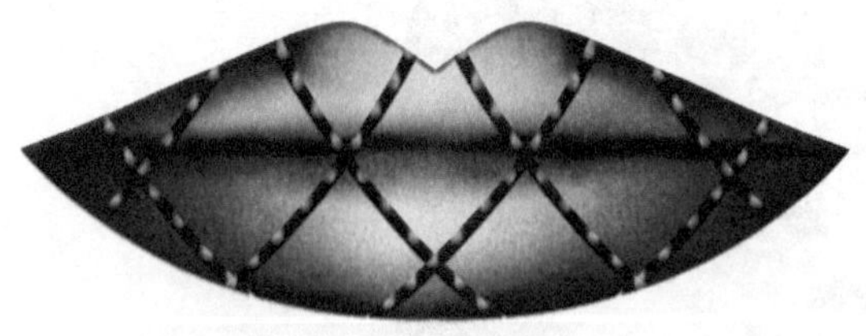

Torn Down

The pure and the virginal are craved by those vulgarly longing to be
the first
The first to take and to taste, to then brandish a medal of gold,
boasting to all
The lustful and the wanton are shamed and objectified in the same
quick breath
They are spoken about freely with the crudest tongues, for they must
not mind
The uninhibited must be accepting of every touch thrust upon them
every day
It is too far-fetched to believe they only feel desire when it is on their
own terms

But whether you are chaste or salacious, it only matters that you are a
woman
For men may do whatever they please, as often as they please, and be
rewarded
How valiant it is to be a man, how easy it is for them to be born into
this world
And immediately reap the rewards of a realm so very insistent on
catering to them

Cover your body from head to toe or display it fully, for it does
not much matter
The sun will still emerge each day, and it will shine its light down
 upon all men
Giving them the deadly strength that they need to steal and spit
and speculate
Brashly, building themselves up, while women are torn down in
 the process

Controlled

How oppressive, how stifling, how unjust
To be a woman in this world—in any world
We are controlled by men with every step
We wearily take throughout this long life
Men who want to grab, to seize, to enter
And cannot fathom the idea of stopping
They will take until we become puppets
Marionettes doing only as they tell us to
To feel only their hands upon our bodies
To hear only their commands in our ears
Men will seek to control our every string
To move us around to their lustful liking
To break our bones so we are arranged
Perfectly on the ground, ready for them
With broken wrists and with bruised hips
They hope we will simply stop resisting
We will stop pulling our strings so taut
Fall to the floor, a pile of shattered limbs
Heavy with the woeful weight of failure
Our sore minds will be graciously empty
As we bleakly wait to be told what to do
Though somehow we will still be certain
That we do not have to do anything at all
For it will simply be done *to* us, always

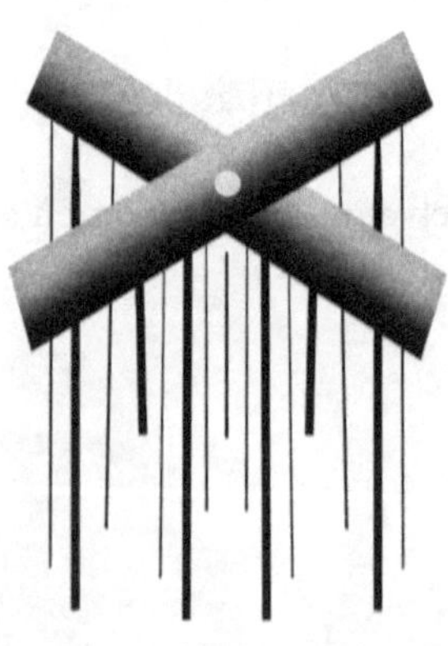

Hypersexualized

Hypersexualized in the way my body merely existed
Exploited as often as tree branches sway in the wind
Undeniably used and underestimated and undervalued
Yet men could easily describe the shape of my body
From memory after a single long and leering look

Feeling eyes constantly watching, staring intently
As if looking hard enough might grant permission
Might allow access to something that is not theirs
Their stares make me feel dehumanized, degraded
An object, a toy, void of any feelings or thoughts
Something incapable of objecting to their pleas

Though I am treated as nothing, I am still alive
I still wear my hair down, letting it cover my neck
For I do not want men to know that I have a pulse
I do not want them to be tempted by the life
That is throbbing beneath my throat, for I know
That they are certain to think it belongs to them

I am not showing off my body, not displaying it
I merely have a body that you choose to look at
My skin does not shimmer for your own pleasure
It is simply rays of the sun beating down upon me
I do not tailor myself for you; I do not think of you
I do not look at you, so please, stop looking at me

My Body

As I grew older I began to realize with horror
That I have no ownership over my own body
How can I keep living in this body of mine
How can I care for it, admire it, nourish it
When it does not completely belong to me
I will not tend to a garden with devotion
Only for someone to storm onto the soil
And rip out every flower from the ground
Leaving destruction and sorrow in their wake

Sometimes I feel myself growing detached
Almost like I am a stranger in my own skin
People are always touching and controlling
As if my body is nothing but an empty vessel
To be brutally used, abused, and discarded
Shivering, wanting to escape from myself
Shaking, trying to be rid of the indentations
That everyone eventually leaves on my skin
I crave the control I once thought I retained
Wishing for power that should belong to me
And yet I fear that power will never come

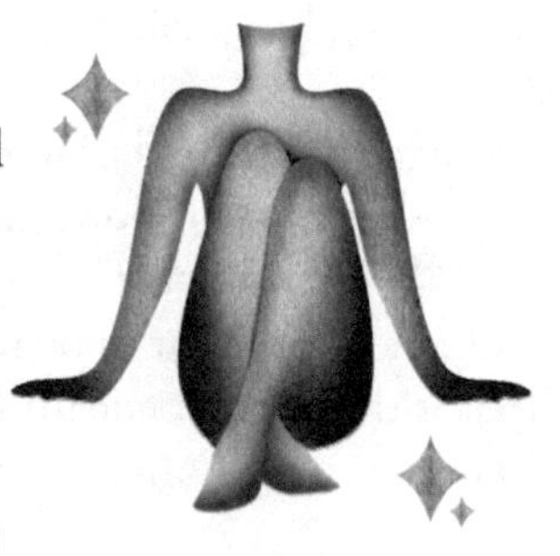

Never in this life will I know true autonomy
Independence and authority over my own skin
And that is sadder than any love story I could pen
I mourn for the women who have come before me
I cry for the women with whom I stand beside today
And I dream of a better life for the women of the future
I hope you are all able to tend to your gardens in peace

Obligation

Do you allow yourself to be touched out of obligation?
For fear of breaking some implicit, unspoken promise?
Their empty eyes are dark with craving while you think
The sooner they are satiated, the sooner I am free to go
Unease hangs heavy in the air, but they can never tell
For that apprehensive aura never wraps around them
It never suffocates them, choking them with such worry
Sometimes you cannot decipher if you enjoy their touch
If their flesh feels heavenly upon yours or akin to hell
For every touch feels as though it is only for their benefit
Their pleasure, at the cost of your autonomy, your will
But then there are times when you *know* with certainty
That their hands will feel like deadly acid on your skin
You will look up and see the impatient intent in their gaze
A gaze that feels binding—that stops you in your tracks
Shuts your mind down, settling into an unthinking state
Knowing what they desire will happen, wanted or not
Hoping that whatever they want, whatever they need
They will take it quickly so you can be alone again
The fear of violence and cruelty clouds your thoughts
Until you are unable to say the words that you long to
Frenzied, you decide to submit to their impending touch
Accepting the venomous feel of their hands on your body
Deciding before they decide first, taking away your choice
Leaving you caught off guard to be violated, hurt, tortured
In times like these, your body does not feel like your own
It feels like something you are handing over for the night
Only to return to yourself when dawn fortunately breaks
Illuminating your body as bloodied, bruised, and broken

Violent Ends

Violent ends begin with violent men
Lies linger; words sting; fists form
Until the cycle begins once again
Men, ever the heroes, the saviors
Dubbed so by their very own hands
These cold-blooded, venomous men
Act with bones that are cast in ice
And think with heat on their minds
They will swiftly steal your warmth
Suck you dry until you are shaking
They will cling to you like a leech
Taking and taking and taking more
While their eyes roll back in pleasure
Once their blood runs as hot as a flame
They will roughly push you to the floor
Unable to consume any more heat
Not that you had any left to offer
The ice in their bones will thaw
And their new fire will fuel them
Leaving you shivering and empty

It is no wonder at all that shadows frighten me less than real men do
Fearful to think I am more afraid of running into a man in the darkness
Than I am of a wild and feral animal; although sometimes it is difficult
To tell the difference between them; it is as if I am walking in the woods
Counting down every last second until I reach shelter, until I am safe
This world is full of lethal predators, treating everyone else as meek prey
Though these predators *choose* evil; they look it in the eye, inviting it in
Welcoming it warmly and fondly, knowing the fear they will incite
Aware of the pain they will cause and not deigning to pretend to care

Rage

Even the cosmos could not withstand the magnitude of our permanent
rage
Such boiling anger threatening to break free, burst from our bodies, run
rampant
All of the unwanted touches and the placating looks and the controlling
words
Simmered under the surface, turning our blood hot, though we did not
complain
We used that fire to halt our cowering, to glisten with the embers now
within us
Our bodies shook with the need to cry, but when we risked opening our
mouths
Screams forced their way out instead, the shrieking sound foreign to our
ears
We thought we were meant to be meek and submissive, but no, not any
longer
Think of the insurmountable fear, the injustices, and horrors of every
single day
And shriek with undiluted fury until even the forgotten gods above hear
you
Proclaim that if our fertile branches are chopped down we will share no
fruit
Declare that if we are treated with malice, only to be condemned and
shamed
Then you will be fated to gaze upon the furious fire within our deter-
mined eyes
And be warned that our flames will easily find you, and our rage will
end you

Circe

Let Circe inspire your soul when you feel slight in the presence of vile men
Invoke her unforgiving ruin upon those who hurt, who take without remorse
Do not ever indulge the heady whims of undeserving and abhorrent men
It is far more rewarding to resign them to a fate just as vile as their actions
Act like animals, and we will gladly turn you into one with a single thought
Feel Circe guide your unwavering hand as you pour poison into a wine glass
Do not dote upon these men, weep at their feet, or worship at their infernal altar
When they would not do the same for you, when they would never even try
Plant your feet rigidly into the soil and speak with steady, calm conviction
Let the many ethereal goddesses of our past move our feet and steel our spines
Hope with everything within you that they watch when we take back control
Call us witches and sorceresses, but heed our spells and understand our magic
Look into our eyes before you burn us; act quick or we will burn you first
Women are more than what we can do for men, what we can offer to them
Men need us much more than they think, while women need only ourselves
Circe and her nymphs thrived independently on their quiet island of solitude
So leave us be, and let us do the same

Fatal Fruit

I would sooner eat a sweet strawberry dipped in poison
Than bend to the will of men with hearts made of stone
If—*when* they treat you like a game, play them right back
Learn their made-up rules and defeat them mercilessly
Wield your softness as a weapon, but do not yet take aim
Wait until your gentle nature has turned sharp and cutting
Disguise yourself; masquerade as weak, fragile, demure
Let them get close enough to help you, to hold you up
Only then can you reveal how fatally wrong they were
Do not feel bad for this deception; do not let it worry you
For they would not have helped you with counterfeit care
If they thought that it would not benefit them more

In stunned shock as they realize what you are capable of
That is when you walk away, never to look back on them
Realizing that the more you distance yourself from men
Far from the poisonous, steadfast energy surrounding them
The more the air around you will seem cleaner and crisper
And you will gladly inhale, swallowing down fresh air
You will not feel as though you are walking on a ledge
Waiting for someone to push you off without a thought
Only to pull you back up, readily expecting a thank you
The tense, invisible hands around your neck will relent
And you will not be afraid any longer

Femme Fatale

Serpentine women, see how we move
Hypnotizing siren, listen to our melody
Celestial goddess, gasp at our radiance
Men will look upon our nimble bodies
Becoming mindlessly charmed, spelled
Not noticing at all when we are reborn
As snakes, bursting up from the wet soil
Slithering through the garden that is life
Serpents do not hide their deadly intent
They announce it, openly manipulate it
Moving through life with a lethal surety
With a wicked glimmer in their dark eyes
Scheming, sliding through a field of flowers
Look to the flame; let it teach you to burn
A pretty rose will prick you all the same
Do not mistake it as harmless, innocent
For the spiked thorns hold all the blame
Men sting as bees; women bite as vipers
Their sting will mend; our bite will end
Know your power, wield it, forcefully
Open your mouth and prepare to bite

More

I could have magic of the gods, and I would still worry within
Their power could move through my veins, and I would still cry
Even the most formidable of spells cannot protect me from men
Their skin could burn and blister upon greedily grazing my body
And they would still find a way to place their hands all over me
Their lungs could collapse after kissing my fatal lips even once
And they would still venture to bring their mouths back to mine

I can shout and scream and shriek, and they will muffle my cries
I can walk freely in the light, and they will wait for me in the dark
Though I have the ability to sting, sometimes it is just not enough
They will suck the poison out themselves, spitting the toxins aside
And go straight back to touching me, always demanding more

Dread

The dirt and the soil can sense tragedy
They can feel it deep within their roots
Connected to everyone and everything
They learn of disasters certain to arise
Far before they will ever come to pass
When the ground shakes beneath you
And when the sky darkens completely
Be sure to look around you and wait

Feel a sense of imminent dread
As misery grows from within
Before infecting all it touches
Seeping out of waiting bodies
Polluting the soil and the tide
Until oceans burst with tears
Flowers wilt upon open hands
Trees are birthed from distress

Wind thrashes in grief, in concern
Moonlight whispers of melancholy
Lightning illuminates storm clouds
Creating a violent, daunting scene
Speak vexing words to this realm
And watch all that is flourishing
Slowly and mournfully begin to die
As the ether is flooded with gloom
Watch it drown a forceful death

If soil could weep for you, it would
The dirt understands what will occur
Knows the desolate horror to come
And desperately desires attention
For something terrible will occur
Sooner than you may ever think
Fear that the world may shatter
And wonder if you are next

Refrain of Refusal

Running through secluded woods, branches jutting out to capture her
Trying to trap her in their clutches; panting, she scarcely dodges them
Feeling their rough bark bruise, though she cannot yet slow her stride
Your footsteps grow even louder, and she knows you are close behind
Suddenly she is no longer afraid of ghouls, spirits, and undead creatures
For she knows that you, made of flesh and bone, are far more sinister
She cannot find anywhere to hide as crimson blood runs down her arms
She tried to distance herself from you, knowing it would never be
enough
If she made it to the very edge of the world, she would still feel you
there
Remembering the feel of your frigid skin on hers, the taste of your
mouth
She shudders thinking of you, only to realize she is not just lost in
memory
As your hands wrap around her waist, she is jolted back to this harsh
reality
You haul her backward, the spiked branches now granting you a wide
berth
Allowing you to easily pass by with her struggling body in your arms
You carry her deeper into the woods, an empty place where evil presides
And as you take, take, take, take, she chants a chorus of *no, no, no, no*
Only for the wind to carry away her refrain of refusal, trapped in the
ether
Her weeping pleas disregarded, her whimpers mistaken for heady plea-
sure
When she has nothing more to give, you leave her lying broken in the
dirt
At once she is irrevocably changed, as though you sealed her coffin shut
Placing her far beneath the ground to live with the memory of this
night
While you walk away, savoring the warmth of sunlight upon your skin
Detached, she now feels a faint sense of relief to be alone with the trees
For she prefers their jagged embrace, coarse as it may be, over yours

Weeping Willows

All alone in the forest, she began to cry
Long sobs wreaked havoc on her throat
The trees only gifted her coarse splinters
Their barren branches offered no shelter
The ground would not soak up her tears
As if the dirt knew of the grief they held
Budding flowers recoiled into themselves
Barring her from breathing their floral scent
The woodland animals skittered far away
Trying to flee from her deafening misery
The energetic air became still and silent
Save for the horrific sound of her wailing

All alone, yet she would have felt worse
If anyone bore witness to her downfall
Better to let the forest watch her break
Without grating words or judging eyes
And when the desolate girl is long gone
The plants will grieve as the grass weeps
And the animals will think of her often
Until then she will cry until she cannot
Until her body has no more tears to give
And she will lie down on the forest floor
Dirt in her hair, thorns pricking her skin
Until the ground swallows her whole

The forest will begin to beg her to stay
Pleading to her, merely seconds too late
And the trees will attempt to fall as well
To sink low to the floor to be with her
And as their branches wail in mourning
The trees are granted a new, suitable title
Thus creating the first weeping willows
Rooted in the ground, naturally distraught
Over she who had long ago come to weep
All alone in the solitude of the dark forest

Tragedy

Tragedy aimed its bow at me and shot an arrow of suffering straight into my soul
The world did not notice as I plucked it out quietly, careful not to spill any blood
Standing in horror as the world went on, as the wind did not even change direction
Agonizing, though in silence, for I did not yet know how to let the words out of me
Waiting for my mouth to scream, my feet to move, and yet none of that occurred
Just as the silver stars did nothing but shine and the darkness did nothing but hide

The horrific night came to an end, and as a new day dawned, a fog encircled me
Invisible to all others, while coating me in a cloudy mist of shame, despair, pain
Eventually the heavy haze began seeping inward, penetrating through my flesh
My body started storing the flooding misery in different places, all inside of me
Trying to conceal it within the internal safe that is my organs and my bloodstream
The smoke enveloping me had seemed heavy though I found I was unprepared
For the damaging burden that it would inflict upon my already breaking body

Swiftly I adapted to the intrusions, but soon there was no more room within me
An excess of pain searched in dire need of a place to latch on to, a place to hide
As I began to ache, it made sense that my body hurt as much as my soul did
For my body was no longer capable of repressing everything so deeply within
The surrounding mist grew thicker, denser, and I could not hide it any longer
My nose began to bleed a shocking scarlet stream that I did not bother to stop
Bones relentlessly throbbed as my skin became inundated with swollen bruises
Eyes watering from fighting the urge to sleep, the urge to let my mind rest, relax
Migraines, fevers, colds, I tolerated them all as my body tried anything it could
To rid itself of the haunting memories it had misguidedly hidden for so long

Waves of fresh agony rigorously washed over my body, lapping at my wounds
Ripping them open again and again as bright blood gushed from the lacerations
A steady pulse of wretchedness settled into my bones and flowed through my veins
Knowing with tragic certainty that the sharp sting of suffering will come and go
But the dull hurt will always stay with me, evermore embedded into my tired flesh

Forgetting

My broken bones were heavy with the sorrows I sustained
Wishing to wash them until the water ran clear, free of shame
My blood felt thick, gummy with lasting fragments of grief
Wanting any traces of the life I led before to leave my body
To vanish into the night without a trace, without a goodbye
And yet even after cleansing and scrubbing and purifying
After washing the blood off again and again, the pain remained
Nothing could erase the stain that had been placed upon my soul
And as my body began to forget, I feared my mind never would

If I still remembered it all when my body was spotless
Maybe the memories would depart if I descended into the soil
Until dirt lined my fingertips from struggling to bury my past
I would claw at the ground until I did not recognize myself
Hoping I could emerge from the earth as a different person
Someone whose tormenting thoughts would remain deep below

And still I frantically worried that would not work either
To escape thoughts of you, I needed to go to a place so far
So distant, I would have to travel through time to get there
Not stopping until I reached a land you have never touched
A land where you have, so mercifully, never touched *me*

My mind holds onto my past with such fervid willpower
With the resolve of someone who is almost afraid to forget
As though forgetting might lead me back to then, to you
Bringing me back to the same mistakes, the same regrets
And thus the cycle would repeat, only this time around
I might not survive

Unsullied

It took days and months and years to understand what you had done to
me
Maybe I should have been collecting my tears all this time to return to
you
For they were birthed from your brutality, from your inhumanity, after
all
I weep for what you had stolen from me, for what I had endured as a
result
Only now am I able to grasp how much you took—how broken you
left me

I still grow nauseated, gagging with sickness at the very thought of you
Someone spoke your name, and I flinched so violently, the ground
shook
Though you are long gone, at least I know that you can never haunt me
For I have always been more of a ghost than you ever were, even now
You may be a spirit, though my empty body has long since been hollow
And wrapping my arms around myself does so little to console my woe
For my skin still crawls and my body no longer feels like it is my own

Peeling the skin off my lips so nothing that you touched will remain
Blood coats my fingers, yet my mouth exhales in relief, in exhaustion
The rest of my body itches with the same urgency, begging to be freed
To shed the flesh that now feels haunted by the branding of your touch
Ripping myself apart until I am red and raw, with only my bones ex-
posed
Then stepping into an unsullied body, one you have never laid yours
upon

Bonded in Misery

Oh, I did not know the hurt would remain for this long
I did not realize it would become this scar on my heart
Every time my heart beats now, it moves with the wound
It moves through the pain, draining me, exhausting me
And I am forced to carry it, to feel it with every breath
Wondering if I need the scar now, if I need it to survive

Times passes, and I wait and wait for the pain to lessen
To subside like a harsh winter falling into a quiet spring
Instead the hurt grows, spreading throughout my body
And every day my stomach hurts and my abdomen aches
Every day I harbor more resentment toward my body
Cursing it for holding on to the pain of trauma so intently

My anguish latches onto my wounded soul like a parasite
Sucking until any hope that the hurt will depart is long gone
Resigning myself to the tragically heartbreaking knowledge
That I will have to live with this pain for the rest of my days
For it is so ingrained into my very being, my very essence
That I cannot live without it, and it cannot live without me
We are one, shaking in agony, bonded in misery, forever

Bloodied Roses

Glide across the tranquil, cerulean river
Reach the quiet meadow just up ahead
Pluck every last bone within your body
Use each as a bridge to make your trip
Watch them float easily atop the water
Glad to be freed from your aching body

Create a bouquet; make it as lovely as it can be
Prick your finger upon a rose; watch it bleed
Use your blood to paint the white roses red
Marvel at the color that was once within you
Notice how it looks better atop the flowers
Than it ever did beneath your skin

Lie in the rain and watch the storm in shock
Think of the bloodied roses, soaked, sodden
Dig your nails down into your pristine flesh
Watch blood pool atop your impaled thighs
The crimson color so familiar to you now
Do not stare in a sullen trance for too long
Or you may never want to look away again

Devastation

The devastation of my body was created by my own hand
My skin bears the wet imprints of my own punishing teeth
Pulling my hair until I held the broken strands in my hands
Clawing and slashing at my stomach with sharpened nails
As if I would be free of this pain if I tore myself open
Sleep struggles to find me, nervous of what it might find
When it stumbles across my destructive, hollow thoughts
If my drowsy eyes begin to close, I force them open wide
Satisfied to see the deep, dark circles in the light of day
Filling my body with acid, reveling in the deadly pain
My body carries just as many dark secrets as my mind
The bruises say more than my mouth could ever express
Cutting my skin open, whispering my mysteries to the gashes
Hoping they will sink into my flesh and swim beside my blood
Until I am weighed down by the control of my own thoughts
Poison of my own creation flowing through my bloodstream
Every word within my mind darkens the color of my veins
Until my insides are as black and soulless as my heart feels
Feeling the urge to break myself open, spilling blood and bones
As if the only way to get the bad out is by sacrificing the good
If there is any good left within me after all I have experienced
Consumed by the yearning to tear my heart from my chest
Giving in, gnawing at flesh until the organ rests in my arms
Tattered, falling apart at the seams, broken by my own woe
Yet, like Prometheus's tired liver, it grows back each day
I wake up feeling it beating within my skin, and I weep
When our minds are crowded with secrets and memories
Daring to overwhelm, threatening to devour us in one bite
We then turn toward our bodies, so enticingly unblemished
We wound, we wail, and we tie our bloodied hands together
Afraid of what we would make them do to us if ever freed
For we have no more skin to bruise, no more blood to spill
Such graceful and lithe fingers, capable of such awful acts
Our bodies are so regrettably cursed with the power to hurt
How tragic it is when we use that power on ourselves

Sadistic Pleasure

Lemon juice stung as it reached her cut; she relished in the feeling of discomfort
The acidic pain was virulent; better to focus on the hurt than what lies beyond
Her mind only ceased its relentless attack with every cut, every bit, every bruise
Pain tasted like opium in her mouth and felt like sadistic pleasure upon her skin
Engulfing her in mindless euphoria, stars in her eyes, dizzy, head spinning, shaking
Legs quivering, heart racing, hands itching with the desire for more pain, more hurt

Though the wounds do not cure her; they do not erase her sickening memories
She does not find any beauty in the ache, though she does find solace in the sting
At least this pain—dark and damaged and discolored—she can see and feel and touch
It is the invisible pain within her mind that she cannot yet bear to face, to confront
Gut her; hack her appendages apart, but do not question the liberating look in her eyes
For when her body is destroyed, her mind will become astonishingly silent at last

Torment

God, my head hurts all the time; the throbbing seems everlasting
The ache is razor sharp, cutting into my skull with a grueling resolve
Nausea rolls through my body, the pain threatening to make me sick
My body burns up in protest, wishing the pain would soon disappear

I deprived my body of everything it begged for: nourishment, kindness
And instead indulged in malicious pain until it demolished me entirely
Starved for gentle compassion while my skin and soul paid the price

Tar filled my veins; ash crowded my lungs; dust settled atop my heart
My body was decaying, rotting; I could not seem to stop it fast enough
My mind began to beg along with my body, and my fear began to grow
I knew the terrible ache clouding my thoughts should not go unheeded

It would greedily grow, multiply, begging for more space to occupy
It would not stop until nothing is left of me but a bleak hopelessness
Once, I reveled in the anguish, yet now I fear the pain will never end
I would gladly sell my soul for a moment of reprieve from this torment

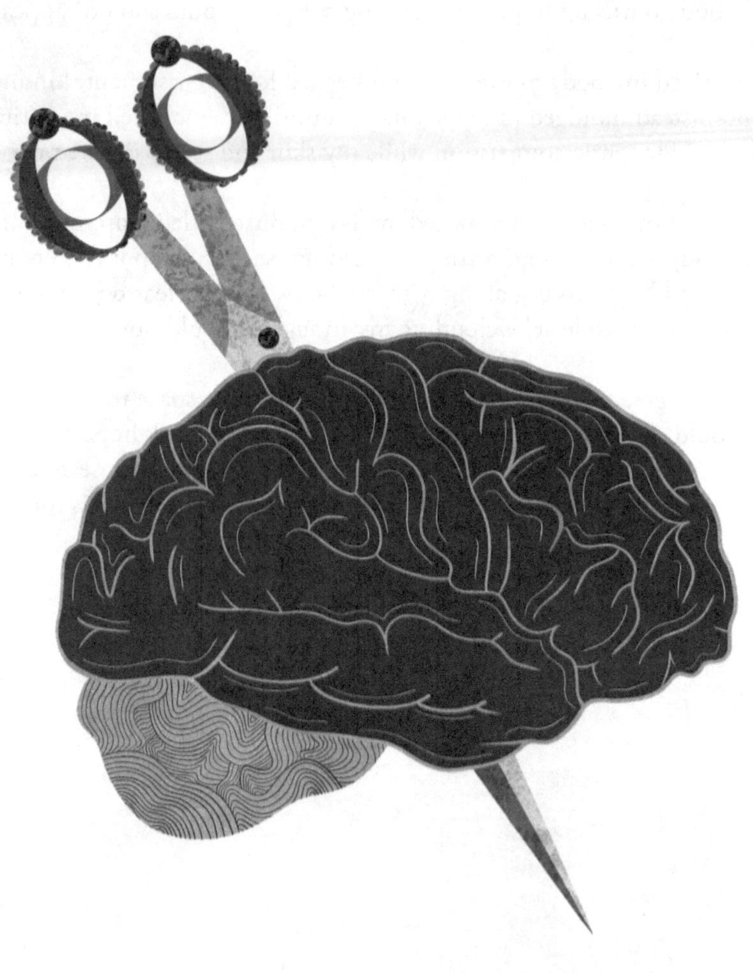

Despair

It had been a long day, but an even longer night and an unbearable year
Minutes had turned to hours, each second more agonizing than the last
I had bled all that I could bleed, and still my grief somehow remained
The pain did not help me forget, so I turned to dismal despair instead
With a traumatized body and an exhausted mind, I began to weep and
weep
As I tasted the tears cascading into my mouth, I relished in the salty
taste
Feeling solace in the fact that I can in fact feel something other than
pain

Brief relief washed over me; the feeling of anguish had become too
frequent
Despair now walked closely beside me, shoulder to shoulder, hand in
mine
It stole the flush in my cheeks, the luster in my hair, the warmth in my
skin
When my knees buckled and I knew that I would soon splinter into
pieces
Despair laid me down peacefully, coaxing more tears from my heavy
eyes
As it begged me to never stop crying, I supposed that I never truly
would

Desolate Day

Languid mornings, rain falling as a fine mist
Curtains open, revealing a miserable dawn
Pressing my face against the freezing window
Feeling the harsh bite of frost upon my cheeks
Hoping the chill in the air would seep into me
Mercifully replacing my warm, emotional heart
With a new heart of ice, devoid of all feeling
At least then, the only pain that I would feel
Would be the cold, callous air coating my flesh
And that—a small sting of ice—I could manage

Later the boiling sun began to beam down upon me
Wincing, I tried to shut my curtains quickly, forcefully
Cursing any tendrils of light attempting to sneak past
Warming the once frosty air, denying me of the chill
Sunlight crept onto my face, illuminating my distress
The hummingbirds noticed, and their singing grew quiet
For the sweeter the day, the more my sorrow will grow
Creeping up my sore throat until I can no longer breathe

The somber sunlight soon became too much to bear
It had set my heart on fire, shrouding it in black char
Misery hungrily latched on to this internal destruction
Willing my body and my soul and my heart to break
One more tear and I would surely dissolve into ash
Each day I waited for my burnt heart to breakdown
And every night I wept when it continued to beat
Despite my darkest desires, my body did not fail
The most I could do was close my curtains tighter
And wait for each desolate day to come to an end

Crescent Moon

Waiting for the severe light of day to soon dissolve
Hoping the silver shade of moonlight might soothe
In the darkness, despair needs not to hide or cower
Shadows lurking within the emptiness understand
Recognizing the shadows living in throbbing minds
Urging us to look up to the night sky, so full of stars

Stars that always see and hear all who need company
All those who feel the most alone as soon as night falls
They work in tandem with the beaming moon to listen
Hearing our mournful cries, they will weep themselves
Knowing that they cannot ease this painful suffering
For they are too far to hold those in dire need of touch
For they are too far to utter calming words of comfort
They do not know that their mere presence is enough

Weep, take solace knowing the sky sheds tears as well
Despair will linger and endure and always remain
Though night is certain to emerge, without a doubt
And it is more capable of empathy, of understanding
Than any person in this world could ever hope to be
When torture threatens to devour us in one final bite
Look to the crescent moon and speak of your agony
In hopes that whispering those words up to the sky
Will lessen their crushing weight, if only for a time

Ocean

Despairing and despondent, she held her breath and walked into the
ocean
Seashells sliced her soles, the red hue diluted into a softer shade from
the waves
The salty seawater twisted around her ankles as she kept walking and
wading
Until she could no longer feel the hot sand from the beach between her
toes
Letting the water pull her under, each wave pushing her further down,
down
Slipping easily under the waves as they washed over her aggrieved body

Her mourning let her sink further and further, with no desire at all for
fresh air
No craving to break the surface and cough up the volume of water in
her lungs
Words of agony died upon her lips, sliding, slipping, sailing back down
And as she opened her mouth once more, daring to part her lips and
speak
It was no longer to lament but to further invite the ocean to consume
her
She took heaping gulps of water, desperately needing her throat to burn
Wanting her lungs to choke under the building pressure of the vast
ocean

She urged her body to sink and begged the sea to hold her, keep her
captive
So she could live among the sea nymphs and the creatures of the frigid
water
She longed to reach the bottom, as if she could not get far enough from
land
Far enough from the golden beach, the warm sand, the setting sun high
above
Letting the water envelop her; feeling cold, her mind cleared, her eyes
closed

Her pulse slowed and she became one with the steady current guiding the sea

The sky and the sun and the wind all seemed so distant, so remote to her now

The water hid her from the world above as the flow of the waves guided her

Allowing her to travel deeper, deeper, until she felt the bottom of the ocean

Feeling free enough to exhale, she gave herself over to the comforting tide

No one could hurt her here, not even herself, not within the shelter of the sea

For she belonged only to the water now, who would protect her, always

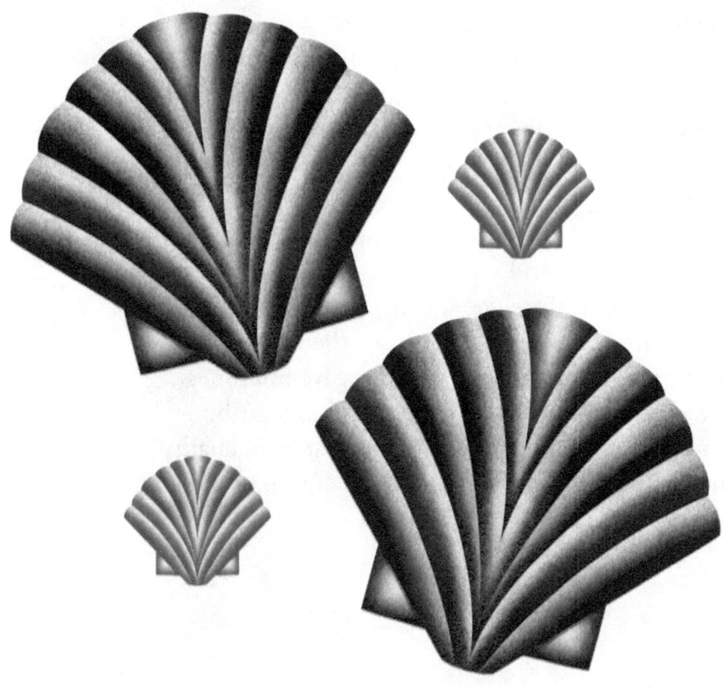

Numb

Aching mind, fatigued limbs, eyes fluttering closed
Headache—no—head is bursting, hiding so much woe
Pain shoots through your skull as a sick punishment
Break me open, *let me out*, your mind is begging you
Though you refuse, and more pain obediently follows
Weep until your throat is tender and tired and raw
The pain never relents as your eyes and nose bleed
Try to scream, though only blood begins to pour out
Too much, not enough; you feel pressure, swelling

You are sure that you will disintegrate into nothing
If the aches you live with do not vanish into the air
If your blood will not stop flowing out like black tar
Dark, like the decaying rot spreading in your mind
It needs to escape, but you are too tired, sore, weak
You want to close your eyes, but the pain is constant
It will not be ignored any longer; it demands to be seen
Your body cannot move; your words cannot be spoken
Not until your suffering is expelled without any guilt

You open your eyes, force them to stay awake, alert
And you fight and fight and fight until the blood clots
Until the pain dulls and your mind is empty and clear
Legs give out, and there you lay, crumpled on the floor
Dismal agony thawing, melting away, then changing
Transforming into a vapor of unresponsive numbness
Which wastes no time in wrapping around your body
Your muscles relax, body slipping into a state of apathy
No more tears, no more pain, no more anything at all

Apathetic

I was destroyed, torn apart, ripped open, then reborn, mind clear, heart empty
After my devastation, any lingering compassion and understanding died within me
I had awoken apathetic with the eyes of a devil, dark and soulless, unsympathetic
Winter had long ago ended, yet the ice in my veins remained, stronger now than ever
My sadness froze over until nothing but a lethargic sense of unconcern was left behind
I spent hours lazing atop the cold tile floor, my hair splayed out around me like Medusa
Feeling as if I had turned myself into stone—into a ghost: my lips blue, flesh untouched
Walking through walls like a spirit, shuddering when my body passed easily through brick
Moving through life as a zombie, life dripping off of my body with every step that I took
My life, my vivacity was better off on the ground, capable of making the flowers bloom
It was of no use to me any longer, for my soul had resigned itself to a life of nonexistence
The flowers grew an inch but began to wilt just as quickly as they had once sprung to life
As if they knew that the life they drank was not theirs, and they could not bear to steal it
Still my lifeless body carried on living, beating, and breathing, though it meant nothing
Just because your heart beats loudly does not mean it loves or feels or aches within you
Just as rivers will flow with no intention and mountains will lead to nothing but empty air
And so, like the rivers and mountains surrounding me, I continued on; alive, but just barely

Well of Indifference

For a world covered in meadows of flora and fauna
So many thorns have found their way into my soul
Poking, stabbing at my heart until I lose all feeling
When the thorns begin to wither away over time
And my heart overflows, once again ready to burst
I swiftly drink from the hollow well of indifference
Anesthetizing myself before I fall sick with sorrow
Before my dreary despair threatens to drown me
I let absolute, abject apathy coat my body
And it spreads through me like a contagion
Causing my thoughts to seize, my heart to slow
I watch as my misery detaches from my body
And simply floats away, landing upon a cloud
Patiently waiting to be picked up by the wind
Carried far from where my hands can reach it
I wanted to feel less, so now I feel nothing at all
I hold my breath and reach out to touch a flame
Allowing the fire to move freely upon my fingertips
Exhaling deeply only when I feel no burn, no sting
And though I knew that I would never feel again
It was wholly better than what I suffered before

Venom

The vile of venom seemed so appealing, so desirable
Until it sat in front of me, taunting, begging to be drank
I longed, so deep within myself, to end this life I lived
Unsure if I wanted to start again as someone new or not
If reincarnated, I was certain my new body, my new heart
Would still hold on to remnants of my past pain and aches
For there is too much discontent to be wiped away entirely

Plagued with a weeping soul stained with such sorrow
And a broken heart yearning to feel anything but agony
The poison tempts me, yet fear of the unknown stops me
Though that unease, that terror, does not stop me for long
For even if my next life is rife with lingering desolation
It is sure to be better than the dreadful life I endure now
I will not know for sure until I bring the vile to my lips
Feel the liquid coat my tongue, and swallow every drop

Goodbye

Goodbye, for this world is too much and yet not enough
Suffering quietly does not mean a war is not raging inside
Retreating so far into myself, certain I have entered purgatory
Too weak to die, too exhausted to live, a never-ending plight
Sick to my stomach, eyes watering, heart pounding within me
Clenching my fists until my knuckles are bursting with blood
There is only so much unbroken hopelessness I can handle
The toxins flowing through my system burn me intensely
Though it hurts less than the aching anguish within my soul
Trying to escape into my dreams, but my mind is not gentle
Asleep, I torture myself, only to wake, continuing the agony
A vicious cycle of distress wrapped up within a miserable life
Perhaps the next will be better; I suppose I will soon find out

Halfway

Fall into a deep sleep, not quite alive, not yet gone
Lose consciousness, body tumbling through space
Descend into another realm, only for a brief moment
Eyes closed in this world and forced open in another
Do not scream; do not worry; do not fear, but do hurry
For any other world is certain to be better than this one

The atmosphere will appear more vivid than ever before
As if every atom that floats through the air is now visible
Water within babbling brooks will sound akin to sonatas
Ears begging for more, eyes entranced by such splendor
Explore this otherworldly nirvana in a hypnotic trance
Rejoice in this realm; linger in this place of in-between

Here, fantasies come true and wishes linger within the seams
Desires are fulfilled, hopes are granted, cravings are satiated
But beyond the tempting beauty, beyond the offer to sleep
To stay in this comatose state and never have to awaken
Comes the overwhelming clarity, the harrowing remorse
And the realization that this idyllic, halfway sort of world
Will have to wait a little while longer to welcome you in

Reborn

Cauterize my wounds; stop the bleeding in my heart
Despite my reluctance to depart, I sunk the knife in
As I wailed, I could not stop myself from forsaking
Until my body was shaking, my soul slipping away
I looked to the moon, eyes begging, as I began to fall

Hold me and touch me and stay with me until the end
Sing to me as I start to drift; anchor me before I vanish
Lure me back toward this life and purge me of my strife
Breathe stardust crafted by an enchantress into my lungs
Let my veins flow with the anecdote of dark divinity

Mark my skin with the words of an ancient witch
Listen as a sorceress whispers to my failing heart
Urging it to beat again with passion and with verve
Wash my hair with the tears of forgotten goddesses

Lay my body beneath a beautiful blue moon, so rare
Watch me return to life, somehow the same, but more
With mystical magic streaming throughout my blood
And bewitching moonlight that sparkles upon my skin
I took a steadying breath and tried to live once more

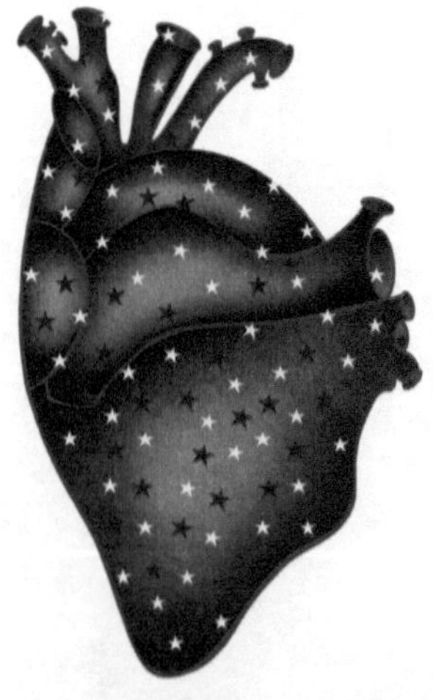

Fantasize

We were fated from birth to grieve, crafted to please
We lived and breathed this torment, never at ease
We have wept and bled and fallen low to the ground
We swallowed our cries so we never made a sound

Though just for tonight, let us fantasize that all is okay
As if we are alone in the world with no one to obey
With no one to please and with no one to pleasure
We may finally breathe at our very own leisure

When dusk emerges, pretend everything is alright
The world is not on fire, it is only the dying daylight
The ground will not collapse; it will not give way
The dirt is merely shifting, pushing the weeds away

The day is finally done; the sunlight is in the past
Our woe is now forgotten; our pain is gone at last
Deeply inhale the crisp air and try to simply *be*
Look up to the cosmos and the stars that are free

Delight in the delicate glow that is the moonlight
Seeping into our bodies, so beautiful and so bright
Savor this dream world, for it will not last too long
Though a life free from misery is where we belong

When the fantasy ends and reality suddenly appears
Where will we go when the void of darkness clears?
When the sun emerges once more, what will we do?
We will live and suffer and try to make it through

Acknowledgements

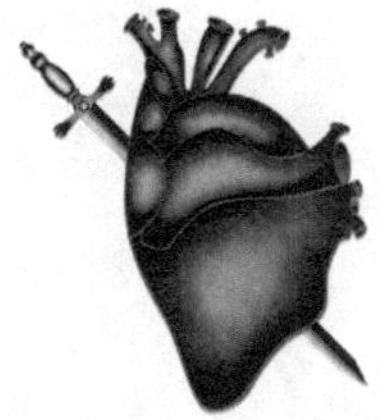

Thank you to my editor, Hope Houtwed, for all of your detailed and insightful edits. I am so grateful to have been able to work with you, and feel immensely appreciative of all the advice you offered!

Special thanks to S.T. Gibson for allowing me to use a quote from her captivating and heady novel, *A Dowry of Blood*, as an epigraph to begin my book. It is an honor to have my work feature a quote by an author whom I admire so much!

Lastly, my deepest thanks to anyone who has decided to read *Midnight Love Potion*, my debut poetry collection! I hope you enjoy it and that the poetry within stays with you long after you close this book.

Marisa Loretta is an author and artist living in Upstate New York. *Midnight Love Potion* is her debut collection of illustrated poetry and prose. Marisa has always been an avid reader, and her love of all things fantasy and romance has only grown over the years. You can find her at www.marisaloretta.com or on Instagram: @marisaloretta

www.ingramcontent.com/pod-product-compliance
Lightning Source LLC
Chambersburg PA
CBHW021148310726
48971CB00002B/542